CHASING
THE
DRAGON

NICHOLAS KAUFMANN

ChiZine Publications

FIRST EDITION

Chasing the Dragon © 2009 by Nicholas Kaufmann
Jacket artwork © 2009 by Erik Mohr
All Rights Reserved.

CIP data available upon request.

CHIZINE PUBLICATIONS
Toronto, Canada
www.chizinepub.com
info@chizinepub.com

Edited by Brett Alexander Savory
Copyedited and proofread by Sandra Kasturi

For Lee Thomas and Stefan Petrucha, dear friends in absentia.

Special thanks to the Who Wants Cake team for all their help with this novella: Daniel Braum, M.M. De Voe, Rhodi Hawk, Sarah Langan, Victor LaValle, K.Z. Perry and David Wellington.

1.

SHE SPEAKS THROUGH THE DEAD

It would be a massacre. It always was. Georgia Quincey had seen it enough times, had witnessed more butchery and blood at the age of twenty-five than most people saw in a lifetime. Pulling her car into the parking lot of the roadside diner, she already knew what kind of slaughter she would find inside. The visions had shown her.

She'd been driving west all day, trying to pick up the Dragon's trail, and somewhere on the dusty plains between Santa Rosa and Albuquerque the visions had come. Terrifying flashes of carnage, so strong she'd had to pull to the side of the road; screaming faces and geysers of blood, the wet rip of shredding flesh, the snapping of bone, and she knew. The Dragon had killed again.

The diner, or what was left of it, stood like the last defiant outpost of civilization in the middle of a vast, arid flatland peppered with Emory oaks and Apache pines. She opened the car door and stepped out into the stifling air. Waves of heat rose off the blacktop and shimmered like spirits. The diner's windows were cracked and painted in red, messy arcs where the blood had hit. The screen door hung off its hinges, banging against the wall in the hot New Mexico breeze. A long fissure cut the pavement like a lightning bolt between the building and the base of a tall metal signpost beside the parking lot, which now tilted toward the ground at an almost forty-five degree angle, half the letters of its flickering neon sign shattered: BET Y'S ROADS DE DINER A G EAT PLACE FO BURG S YOU BETCHA! Half a dozen empty cars waited in the parking lot, their engines ticking in the heat, but there were no people. No survivors. There never were. No one who'd been inside when the Dragon came calling had stood a chance.

Please, she thought, *don't let any of them still be moving.* Dead bodies were something she didn't think she'd ever get used to, especially after the Dragon had feasted on them, but the ones that still walked, those were the ones that really wigged her out. Those were the ones she had to be careful of.

Georgia stretched, cracked her back, and pulled the pump-action shotgun from the backseat.

She approached the diner slowly, careful to step around the enormous crack in the pavement. Concrete crumbled at the edges of the fissure, and smaller cracks were already starting to form, branching out into the parking lot. It wouldn't be long before the whole structure collapsed. The sound of her boots crunching over the gravel put her in mind of *High Noon*, her father's favourite movie. Something about the image of the lone protector, the hero no one would—or could—help, had resonated strongly with him, and he'd shown it to her dozens of times. She imagined herself for a moment as Gary Cooper headed alone to the showdown with Ian McDonald. All she was missing were jangling spurs on her heels.

She forced the thought from her mind. The truth wasn't glamourous like a movie. The truth was bald and ugly. Forgetting that would get her killed.

She watched the diner's windows and listened for sounds of movement, but there was only the low moan of the desert wind blowing across the flatlands. The screen door banging.

She gripped the shotgun tight and stepped inside. She noticed the coppery smell of spilled blood the moment she stepped over the threshold. The heat released from the eviscerated bodies made the air humid despite the rattling air conditioner over the door. A bank of booths ran along the wall on her right, all the way to the swinging doors of the kitchen. Blood dripped from the windows, ran along the tabletops and trickled off the edges like spilled cola. The floors, the seats were littered with bones and chunks of bloody meat—pieces of the Dragon's victims. Georgia saw the stump of a stockinged leg, a high-heeled shoe still on the foot, and turned away to keep her gorge from rising. At the counter, six stools were bolted to the floor, each spattered with blood and grue. An array of cracked plates and smashed coffee mugs cluttered the countertop, and at the far end, half a human torso sat like an order of steak waiting to be brought to a table, its one remaining arm still inside the sleeve of a shredded blue Oxford. Beyond it, the dessert rack creaked on rusty gears, the pies and cakes spinning in lazy, indifferent circles.

The building shuddered around her. Cracks split the black and white linoleum floor. There wasn't much time.

She stepped deeper inside and wondered if the Dragon was still there, hiding, waiting for Georgia to let her guard down. It had taken her half an hour to find the diner after the vision hit. The Dragon could already be long gone. But she had to be sure.

The floor buckled and leaned. A severed arm rolled against her foot. The hand landed on her ankle, the fingers brushing her skin. She bit back a yelp and kicked it away.

The heavy clang of a pan falling in the kitchen made Georgia jump. She lifted the shotgun to her shoulder and turned to the swinging doors.

The doors banged open and a hulking form stumbled out—fat, moustached, wearing a grease-stained apron. A fry cook, or it had been once. Both the apron and the shirt beneath had been torn open, revealing deep gashes in its chest and stomach. Blood oozed over grey skin, thick black veins. It came toward her with jerking, awkward steps, its dead muscles lacking the coordination to walk properly.

It fixed her with milky white eyes, opened its cracked black lips and said, "I was wondering when you would come."

Its voice was deep, dusty and undeniably female. The Dragon's voice.

Georgia grit her teeth and tried to keep the heebie-jeebies under control. The talking corpses made her skin crawl every time. She had to remind herself the thing in front of her wasn't human, wasn't even alive in any sense of the word. The Dragon was controlling its movements, speaking through its mouth.

The dead made a perfect and lethal army, unwavering, unquestioning, unstoppable so long as the brain remained intact to operate the motor functions. Georgia's father had called them ghouls, but she had her own name for them. Something she thought was more fitting.

Meat puppets.

Instead of attacking her, the meat puppet tilted its head in puzzled amusement, and the Dragon said through it, "You should be dead, child. You should have died when I tore you open. Yet here we are. Together again."

Georgia pumped a shell into the shotgun's firing chamber. "You must he disappointed."

The corpse laughed, a horrible sound. "Disappointed? No, child, I am intrigued. For centuries I have triumphed over the warriors who stood against me. Tore them open like ragdolls. Devoured them while the life drained from their eyes. But you, child. You are different. When I opened you, your blood stung me. It burned. When I opened you, you *lived*. I find this remarkable. It has been such a long time since I have had a challenge."

Georgia smirked. If there was one thing she knew about

the Dragon, it was that she loved the sound of her own voice. "If you're so confident, why don't you face me yourself? Why hide and make this *thing* do your dirty work?"

The meat puppet stepped toward her. She sighted down the barrel at its head, but her hands shook. *Come on, girl, get it together*, she thought. *You've done this plenty of times.*

"We are not dissimilar, you and I," it said. "It seems neither of us dies easily. Devouring you will be all the sweeter for it."

"Where are you?" Georgia demanded. "You want to kill me so badly? Tell me where to go. Tell me where to find you."

"I am everywhere, child. I am all around you." Grey, rigid arms wrapped suddenly around her from behind, one snaking across her stomach, the other hooking around her neck. Another meat puppet had sneaked up on her while she'd been distracted. Georgia cursed her own incompetence. The arms pulled her back, and she tripped, banging her head against the floor. The shotgun accidentally discharged, shattering one of the windows, and the recoil knocked the weapon out of her grasp.

The meat puppet fell on top of her, a middle-aged woman with thick red viscera poking wetly out of a torn flowered dress. It scrambled for a hold, pinning her legs and one of her arms. With her free arm, Georgia reached for the shotgun, her fingers barely grazing the recoil pad at the end of the stock. The meat puppet reached for her neck. Georgia struggled for the shotgun again. This time she was able to grab hold of the stock and pull it toward her. As the meat puppet's hand wrapped around her throat, Georgia swung the shotgun up and shoved the barrel under its chin. She squeezed the trigger.

Nothing happened.

Dammit! She hadn't ejected the first shell. The next one wasn't even in the firing chamber yet. With one arm pinned, she couldn't work the pump. Panicking, struggling for air as dead hands tightened on her throat, her gaze fell on the table in the booth next to her, its metal legs bolted into the floor. Georgia jammed the fore-end of the shotgun pump against one leg and pushed with all her might. Everything grew dim. In another minute, she would lose consciousness. In two, she'd be dead. She gave one last push, and the fore-end finally slid back against the counterpressure of the table leg. The spent shell tumbled out of the ejection port, and a second clicked into place in the firing chamber.

Another tremor rocked the building. Plaster dust rained down from a crack that appeared in the ceiling. The meat puppet fell off of her. Gasping to pull air into her lungs, Georgia rolled away, came up on her knees, and levelled the shotgun at its head.

It didn't bother getting up off the floor. It turned its filmy eyes to her and snarled, "Like a ragdoll."

Georgia pulled the trigger. With a loud bang that rang in her ears, the shotgun jerked against her shoulder and the corpse's head turned into a wet red stain on the floor.

She spun around. The other meat puppet, the fry cook, stood by the counter. It pulled a steak knife out from beneath the broken plates and turned to her. Georgia pumped the shotgun, sending the hot shell clattering to the floor.

The meat puppet paused. It was outmatched, too far away for the knife to be of any use. "You want to know where I am?" it said. "I am closer than you think."

"Whatever," Georgia said, lifting the shotgun. "I'll find you. I always do." A crooked smile creased the dead man's face. "Or perhaps, child," the Dragon said, "I will find you." Georgia pulled the trigger. The meat puppet's head exploded in a shower of blood and bone that spattered against the glass of the rotating dessert rack.

The building trembled again and the floor started to sink. She needed to get out of there before the whole place came down on top of her. She quickly scooped up the shotgun shells from the floor and put them in her pocket, just as her father had taught her. Then, stepping over body parts and pools of blood, she walked to where the cash register sat on the counter by the door. She scanned the buttons until she found the No Sale. She hit it, the register dinged and the drawer slid open. She scooped up the bills inside and did a quick count: two hundred and forty dollars. She fished her wallet out of her pocket, opened it.

A small photo in one of the plastic sleeves greeted her. A man with short dark hair and a strawberry-blonde woman, arms around each other's shoulders and smiling in front of a house. A brown spot intersected the edge of the man's forehead where a drop of blood had dried long ago. George and Tanya Quincey, her parents. She stuffed the wad of bills into her wallet, pocketed it, and slid the register drawer closed again.

It shamed her, stealing from the dead like that, but she didn't have a choice. She had no home anymore, no job, but she still needed money for food, for gas and shells and a bed for the night. She hoped the dead understood.

When she left the diner, the sun was a hazy orange ball hovering at the horizon and the desert heat was starting to dissipate. She stopped in the middle of the parking lot and closed her eyes, letting the cool air wash over her. She almost couldn't feel the weight of the shotgun in her hand anymore. There was only silence and a sweet breeze off the flatlands. A moment of calm, of stillness, to let her tense nerves and muscles unwind, that was all she wanted. Blanket peace, she called it. A feeling she remembered from when she was a little girl wrapped in her favourite blanket, the worn, powder blue one with Snoopy peeling off his stitchwork. The same feeling she'd had when her father would pick her up and carry her, her nose nuzzled against his neck with the scent of tobacco and aftershave wrapping around her.

A loud groaning sound broke through the calm. She opened her eyes.

Behind her, wood snapped, metal girders creaked, and the diner's roof sagged inward. The building shifted, part of it sinking halfway into the earth as more deep cracks broke the asphalt of the parking lot. The leaning signpost finally completed its fall, dropping into the trees beyond the lot with a loud crash. Sighing, she walked to her car.

The driver's side door hung open. Georgia was sure she'd closed it. She gripped the shotgun with both hands, looked around for movement, but there was nothing. Inside the car, someone had rummaged through her belongings. Another meat puppet, no doubt, or maybe the same one that had sneaked up behind her in the diner. But why would the Dragon bother with her car? What was she looking for? In the backseat, Georgia's suitcase was open and her clothes were scattered. Her purse had fallen out of the car, its spilled contents fanned out on the pavement. Georgia's heart sped with a sudden panic. She scanned the ground, searching desperately. She knelt and scooped up objects as quickly as she could. A makeup compact, a tampon, a half-empty pack of gum, she shovelled everything back into her purse, but the one thing she needed wasn't there.

"Shit, shit, shit!" She couldn't lose it. She *couldn't*.

And then she spotted it, hidden where it fell behind the front wheel—a brown leather pack, rolled up tight and bound with a leather strap. She snatched it up and sighed with relief.

Georgia climbed into the driver's seat and closed the door, shutting out the world, if only for a moment. She hugged the leather pack to her chest and leaned her head against the steering wheel. It took a moment to fight off the sobs building in her chest, and then she started the car.

2.

SHE TAKES EVERYTHING YOU LOVE

Georgia kept her car on the same road that led from the diner, heading west. All around her, there was nothing but flatland as far as the eye could see. Brown earth stubbled with dry desert shrubs. In the distance, the southern tip of the Rockies jutted up against the seemingly endless sky. The setting sun nestled red and hazy behind the peaks, and as it sank away the sky dimmed to a dark purple. It was only when daylight faded to dusk and she switched on the headlights that she realized hers was the only car on the road. An unexpected loneliness rose inside her. She felt like the last woman on Earth, and suddenly she wanted—no, she *needed*—to see people. Needed to touch another living human being to wipe the memory of dead meat puppet skin from her fingers.

Fifteen miles from the diner, she finally saw signs of

civilization, and her vice-like grip on the steering wheel eased. She hadn't realized she'd been squeezing so hard, and now, feeling foolish, she shook the tension out of her hands and slowed the car. The road took her past what appeared to be an abandoned industrial area comprised of boarded-up warehouses and empty lofts. The streets and sidewalks were empty, but she knew whatever dusty little New Mexico town claimed the warehouses as its own couldn't be much farther.

And then, signs of life. Modest single and bi-level homes appeared alongside the road on patches of dry, brown grass. Cars passed her on the street, children played in yards until their parents called them in for dinner, streetlamps and door-side lanterns switched on as twilight turned to night, and Georgia felt like crying. She felt like throwing open the car door, hugging the nearest person and shouting, "You're alive!"

I've gone mad, she thought, *completely off my rocker*, but she couldn't help grinning at the idea of scaring some bewildered townie with a random display of affection.

The residential neighbourhood eventually gave way to a small downtown area with a movie theatre and little specialty shops lining the sidewalks. A tiny post office stood across from the theatre, the sign over its doors proudly proclaiming the town's name to be Buckshot Hill. It struck her as an odd choice, considering it was built on some of the flattest land she'd ever seen, but she couldn't deny the name had a certain Wild West charm to it.

Downtown Buckshot Hill was teeming with life. She

drove slowly, watching people navigate the sidewalks and get in and out of their cars. Locals out for a carefree night of going to the movies, of pie and coffee, and then it would be home and early to bed, kiss the kids and turn off the light. They didn't know how close the Dragon had come to their little town. How close they'd been to death. How could they? Most of them probably wouldn't hear about the massacre at the diner until tomorrow morning's news, and even then they wouldn't know the truth behind the headline.

The Dragon was her burden and hers alone. She couldn't tell anyone. They'd gape at her like she'd put a cat on her head and proclaimed herself Queen Elizabeth. She'd seen the look before. It had been all over Drew's face the day he walked out on her.

She tried to push Drew from her thoughts, but the scenery wasn't helping. Young couples were everywhere, holding hands while they dashed across the street in front of her, sitting close together at umbrella-topped tables outside the ice cream parlour. Girls looked adoringly into the faces of their high school sweethearts, tossed their freshly brushed and styled hair while their boyfriends pulled colourful varsity jackets around their broad shoulders. Georgia frowned, bit her lip. Drew had owned a similar varsity jacket when they met in college. He told her it belonged to his brother, a high school football star, and that he himself only wore it with a sense of irony, so he'd always remember football stars made more money than philosophy majors. He said it would keep him humble when he eventually won the Nobel. She'd laughed at that, and looking back, she was pretty sure that was the moment she'd stupidly fallen in love with a dorky philosophy major from Topeka with a girlfriend waiting for him back home.

But she'd been nineteen, full of wisdom and certain she knew everything there was to know. She thought she could hang out with him all semester and keep her feelings at bay. But the night they went together to see an excruciating Drama Department production of *Guys and Dolls*, everything changed. It felt like a lifetime ago . . .

They walked out of the campus theatre trying to keep their laughter inside until they got far enough away, but it didn't work. Drew broke first, laughing so hard Georgia thought he was going to cry, and then that made her laugh too. When they caught their breath, she reached out without even knowing why and touched his varsity jacket. She ran a hand over it like it was the finest silk, gripped the hem at his waist and gave it a playful tug. Drew turned, and the next thing she knew, her back was against the wall and Drew was kissing her.

"I hope that was okay," he said, "because I've kind of been wanting to do that for a while. In fact, I kind of want to do it again. A lot. Is that weird?"

"I . . . what . . ." Georgia tried to focus her thoughts. "You have a girlfriend."

Drew leaned close again, propping himself against the wall with one hand. "Not anymore. It wasn't her I wanted to be with. It was you. Right from the start. There's something different about you. I felt it the moment I met you. I don't know what it is, but sometimes I see you across the quad or in class and it's like you're . . . glowing. You're all I can think about, George." George was his nickname for her. She didn't particularly like it because George was also her father's name, but suddenly it sounded kind of cute the way he said it. *"I know this is weird and sudden and crazy, and I wouldn't blame you at all if you never wanted to talk to me again after springing this on you."*

Drew's face was right in front of hers, the tip of his nose touching her cheek, his breath warm across her lips. Their faces were so perfectly aligned that Georgia wasn't sure exactly when they'd begun kissing again, or who'd started it this time, or if it even mattered. She thought it was the most perfect night ever created. A night that had come into being only so this kiss, too, could come into being.

Sitting in her car, watching the kids shout and roughhouse and make out on the sidewalks, Georgia remembered that kiss, remembered a passerby telling them to get a room, and they had, eventually deciding to live together the first year after graduation. But then her parents—

She swallowed hard, pushed away the image of what the Dragon had done to her mother and father.

After that, everything went to hell. Suddenly it was her turn to take up the hunt. The legacy of her forefathers. She had to quit her job at the graphic design firm. She couldn't tell Drew why she'd quit, where she kept disappearing to, or why she would come back sometimes wide-eyed and shaking. He accused her of doing drugs, threatened to leave, and so she told him the truth. She thought he'd believe her the way her mother had believed her father, so she told him about the

Dragon and about who she was and who her ancestors were, and he'd gaped at her like she was the cat-crowned Queen Elizabeth . . .

"You need help, Georgia," he said. Georgia, not George. Drew shook his head. He looked sad, defeated.

"I can't. This is something I have to do alone. It's too dangerous for—"

"No," Drew interrupted. "I mean you need help." And he'd walked out. She never saw him again, only received a terse letter from Topeka telling her to box up his things because a moving company was coming for them.

Orphaned, jobless, alone—there'd been nothing left for her but the chase, and the vast, insurmountable loneliness of knowing she could never share her life with anyone. The Dragon had done that to her. Destroyed her life. Taken away everything that mattered.

Lost in her thoughts, Georgia almost missed the red light at the intersection in front of her. She slammed on the brakes. A young couple had just stepped out into the crosswalk, and when Georgia's car screeched to a halt, the girl sneered at her and the boy flipped her the finger. Charming. A continuous parade of happy young couples passed in front of her, each seemingly happier than the last. Georgia turned away, annoyed, and spotted a man in stained, shabby clothes sitting on the sidewalk beside an ATM vestibule. His hair was long and stringy, a knotted beard drooped off his jaw, and he shook a Dunkin Donuts coffee cup whenever someone walked by. Most kept moving, but a few dropped change into the cup.

The hobo looked in his cup, counting his take. Then

he stood up, scrawny in his oversized clothes, and started walking. Georgia recognized the way his body trembled and shook with each step. The junkie dance. She turned back to the steering wheel just in time to see another young couple staring at her from the curb. Above the crosswalk, the light had turned green.

"Hey, dipshit," the boy called. "You forget how to drive?"

Georgia stepped on the gas and pulled away just as the girl shouted, "Stupid bitch!"

These were the people she risked her life to protect? *You're welcome*, she thought bitterly, then immediately felt guilty. It wasn't their fault. They didn't know.

She needed some rest, that was all. She couldn't remember the last time she'd slept. Little Rock maybe, or Wichita Falls. It was hard to tell. One place was the same as any other when all you did was blow through on the Dragon's trail and hope this wouldn't be the place you died. But after the fight at the diner, what she wanted more than anything was a long hot shower, a nice meal and a comfortable bed. Unfortunately, she would have to make do with a vending machine and a cheap motel with a rock-hard mattress and sandpaper sheets, as usual. At least they usually had showers.

She found a motel on the far side of town, the Buckshot Motor Inn according to the rotating neon sign, though the placard on the office door said BUCKSHOT MOTORIN'. The office was a small room with a pickup truck calendar thumbtacked to the wall, a mostly empty spinning rack of brochures for local tourist attractions, and an empty aquarium that bubbled and churned despite the lack of fish. A boy who couldn't have been more than fifteen years old sat behind the counter, watching a small TV. The boy's face still bore the ravages of teenage acne, his brown hair oily and uncombed. On the TV, a man with a thick moustache and black hat called someone in a saloon a "cocksucker" and pulled a knife. The boy looked up at Georgia and grinned sheepishly, revealing metal braces wired across his teeth.

"Didn't hear you come in," he said, turning down the volume. "My dad doesn't let me watch this show normally, on account of all the swearing and ti . . . uh, nudity, but whenever I get the chance while he's out . . ." He shrugged. "Anyway, what can I do for you, miss? You looking for a room? Guess you must be. No one comes here just to hang out, right?" He smiled again, then closed his mouth quickly, as if suddenly embarrassed by his braces.

"I guess they don't," Georgia said. "I need a room for one night, maybe two. Something with a hot shower and privacy."

"No problem," the boy said. He stood up and walked over to a row of keys hanging on pegs. "All the rooms got hot water, and they all got curtains and locks so no one disturbs you. You, uh, here with someone?" The acne on his cheeks disappeared in a deep blush. "Sorry, I just mean . . ." He closed his eyes and took a deep breath. "Focus, Wilbur. Do it like Dad taught you." He opened his eyes again. "Single occupancy or double?"

"Single," Georgia said, trying not to laugh. It was hard keeping it inside. She hadn't laughed in a long time.

"Any bags?"

"One in the car. I can handle it."

Wilbur took a key off its peg and returned to the counter. "That's thirty-five a night, including tax, and we need the first night's up front," he said. Georgia handed him two twenties still greasy from the diner's cash register. He handed her a five in return and asked her to sign the guest ledger. When she was done, he swung the ledger around to look at her name. "Georgia, huh? Like the state. You from there?" She shook her head. "No, I guess no one from Georgia would be named Georgia. It would just sound silly, wouldn't it? Like, 'I'm Georgia from Georgia,' you know?" He handed her the key, his face burning red with the realization that he was babbling again. "I can show you to your room if you want."

"I can manage. You don't want to miss the rest of your show."

Wilbur nodded. "All right. Room nineteen, like it says on the key chain. Just hit zero on the phone if you need anything. It's just me tonight, but I can, you know," he shrugged, "whatever." He grinned, keeping his lips together this time, but he seemed a little deflated. Poor kid, she thought. She could tell he liked her, even if she had a good decade on him. She could also tell he was shy around girls. She felt bad for him and threw him a smile as she walked out of the office, but he was already engrossed in his TV show again.

She found her room nearly all the way down the long porch from the office. The door had the metal numerals 1 and 9 bolted to the wood, but the 1 was chipped in half and looked more like an apostrophe. She dragged her suitcase into the pitch-black room and switched on the bedside lamp. The bulb flared, flickered and went out. She tapped it lightly, and it flickered again before blowing out for good. Georgia sighed. Sometimes it seemed like the whole world was falling apart around her.

The lamp on the other side of the bed worked, though, and in its light she saw a motel room depressingly similar to every other one she'd stayed at. There was the usual double bed with a floral bedspread way too chipper for the run-down surroundings, a TV whose rabbit ears probably wouldn't pick up anything but static, a dresser with a single drawer and, in the rear, a bathroom whose toilet was so close to the shower stall she wasn't sure she'd be able to sit without banging her knees. But the water was hot and the pressure was good, and as she stood under the shower nozzle and let the spray run through her hair and down her back, she reached for that elusive blanket peace again. She let her mind go blank so that there was only the hot water and the pores of her skin opening like receptive flowers. She tried to imagine what her life would be like if there were no Dragon, if she were just a normal girl sitting outside an ice cream shop and holding someone's hand without a care in the world.

The fantasy didn't last long. As soon she stepped out of the shower and wiped the steam off the mirror, her reflection was there to remind her of the truth. She'd grown thinner. Too thin, her mother would say if she were still alive, and she would be right. Georgia thought she looked as bony as something out of the dinosaur wing of a museum. She could count her ribs through her skin. Her chest, never that big to begin with, now looked positively boyish. Worst of all was the ugly gash in her left hip. She twisted around to get a closer look, touching the skin around it where the rosy pink was tinged with grey.

The Dragon had taken a chunk out of her months ago, the last time they'd met. Mauled her and, for reasons Georgia still didn't understand, ran off instead of finishing the job. She stared at the scar. It had already healed over, no longer the red gaping maw it once had been, but the ragged concavity in her side repulsed and frightened her each time she saw it. She bit back the tears welling in her eyes. The life she'd been born to had already taken whatever hope she had for happiness, cut away everything she'd loved and left her with nothing but the Dragon. Sometimes she wished she had died that day. Then she could have blanket peace forever.

Georgia tied her hair back in a ponytail, put on a t-shirt and sweat shorts, and left the motel room. Outside, the temperature had dropped and the air felt dry and cool. Two vending machines stood on the porch just outside her room, one selling candy bars and bags of nuts, the other selling Coke and bottled water. She bought herself a big bag of cashews and was dropping coins in the second machine for a can of Diet Coke when the door to the adjacent room opened. A pudgy, middle-aged man in a dress shirt and slacks stepped out. A moustache brushed his upper lip, and a ring of tightly curled black hair circled a bald pate the colour of dark chocolate. He closed the door behind him gently and tugged at the open collar of his shirt as if he was used to loosening a tie that wasn't there now. He pulled a cigarette from his breast pocket, then turned to her and gasped.

"Oh, Lord," he said, stepping back with a chuckle. "I didn't see you there, girl. You gave me quite a start."

"Sorry," Georgia said. She pulled the Diet Coke out of the tray at the bottom of the vending machine, popped open the can and, suddenly aware of how thirsty she was, drained half of it in a single go. Her throat complained, still sore from the meat puppet's grasp, but she didn't care. It felt good to drink something. It felt normal.

The man stuck out his hand and said, "Marcus Townsend."

She shook it. "Georgia Quincey."

Marcus nodded, lit his cigarette and gazed at the stars twinkling just above the forest across the street. "Bad night," he said. "Did you hear the news? Terrible."

"Hear what?" Georgia's empty stomach rumbled. She tore open the bag of cashews and popped a handful into her mouth.

"It's all over the news tonight. Something went down at a diner a few miles outside town, back toward the Interstate. The place was robbed, but whoever did it were a bunch of maniacs. A lot of people are dead. Must have been a whole gang of 'em with shotguns and, I don't know, machetes by the sound of it. It was a bloodbath. Must've been on a real rampage because they said even the building was so damaged it was falling apart when the police got there." He shook his head, still staring off into the distance, and muttered, "White people." Then he turned to her and smiled. "No offense. I'm just saying. We don't get this kind of crazy in Detroit. I hope the cops catch the sons of bitches that did it."

They won't, Georgia thought. They wouldn't even know where to start looking. The Dragon kept to the shadows and avoided major population areas. She struck too infrequently, and rarely twice in the same vicinity, to develop a clear MO the authorities could work from. In fact, after Georgia collected her shells, the only solid constants at each scene were her own tire tracks, and it was only by the grace of jurisdictional rivalry and good old-fashioned bureaucratic incompetence that no one had pieced it together yet and put out an APB on her car. Still, her luck had to run out sooner or later. Someone would connect the dots, and then there would be questions, accusations, explanations the police would never believe. And all the while, the Dragon would keep killing.

She shook the thought from her head and figured it was time to change the subject. "What brings you to New Mexico?"

"Business," Marcus said. He sucked on his cigarette and blew smoke up over his head. "I'm in textiles. Artificial fibres, mostly. Polyester, acrylic. I'm heading out to Albuquerque, go there every year for the trade shows, but I brought my boy with me this time 'round. He's old enough now that I thought I'd make a vacation out of it, show him some of the country so he doesn't think it's all high rises and housing projects, you know?" He looked back at the door to his room. "He's sleeping now. Tomorrow we're going to see a rodeo or some shit." He chuckled softly. "What about you?"

"Business," she said, nodding.

He looked her up and down and arched an eyebrow. "Business? You're too young to be going on business trips, girl. What are you, right out of college? Hell, you should be living in a loft in New York with eight other kids trying to figure out what to do with your life, not travelling all over the damn place on business. That's not what being young's about." She didn't say anything, and Marcus looked away. He nodded at her car parked in the spot before her door. "That yours?"

"Yeah."

"It's a Chevy Impala, right? What is it, an '80, '81?"

"I think so," she said. "It used to belong to my dad."

"What was it, his *first* car?" Marcus laughed.

"He liked it," Georgia said. She took another swig from the can, finishing it off. "It runs all right, never gave him any problems. He drove it right up to the day he died."

He frowned. "I'm sorry, I didn't realize he'd passed."

"It was a while ago now."

He took a deep breath and looked at the car again. "I'm a car nut. I love the damn things. I guess everyone in Detroit is born loving 'em. But I never saw an '81 Impala that still ran. No disrespect to your father, but please tell me you inherited more than this old box of bolts."

More than I could possibly explain, she thought.

Georgia tossed the soda can and the empty bag of cashews into a garbage pail next to the vending machines, and nearly doubled over with a sudden cramp like a fist in her gut. *Not now*, she thought, *please*. Her hands trembled. She felt a twinge in her scarred hip, cold and sharp as a knife. Sweat broke out on her forehead, under her arms, rolled down her back. She glanced anxiously at the door to her room.

Sluggish and heavy, she itched everywhere, like fire ants swarming over her skin. She scratched at her arms. The muscles of her back and legs twitched. The cramp in her stomach twisted harder.

Why did it have to be now?

Marcus was looking at her. He'd been talking the whole time and she hadn't heard a word. He said, "You okay?"

She fought down an eruption of panic. Did he know what was happening to her? Would he call the police? She had to get inside. She pictured the brown leather pack sitting in her purse, could already see herself undoing the strap and rolling it open. She backed toward the door.

"I have to go," Georgia said. She chewed her lip. The cramp in her gut was unbearable.

"You sure you're feeling okay? You don't look so good."

"I'm fine," she insisted. She felt the sweat on her forehead rolling toward her eyes and was sure Marcus could see it too, glistening in the porch lights like a beacon. He would know and he would call the police and for years he'd tell the story to his shocked friends and family, his voice thick with disdain, *"I was standing right there with her and didn't even know she was a junkie until she started jonesing. White people."* But instead, he shrugged and said, "You have a good night."

She grunted something—maybe it was "thanks" or "night"—and opened her door a crack. She slid inside like a draft, then slammed it closed again and locked it. Her purse sat on the bed, a smear of dirt scuffing the side where it had fallen on the ground. Georgia attacked it, yanking it open and dumping everything out until the brown leather pack fell into her lap.

She undid the strap, unrolled the pack on the bedspread and did a quick inventory of the contents: an old, rusty spoon, flame-blackened on the bottom; the remains of a jumbo-sized cotton ball that had been picked at for weeks; a pocket lighter; a yellowing plastic syringe, its needle sheathed in a blue cap; and a small zip-locked plastic baggie with a small amount of light brown powder inside. *Less than a quarter of what there used to be*, she thought.

She snatched up the baggie and opened it carefully. She tapped some of it into the spoon, her nerves on edge, worried she'd spill it and waste all that was left. But she'd prepared the fix so often her hands could do it on their own at this point, and before she knew it she was pulling back the plunger and filling the syringe with liquid heroin.

Georgia lay down on the bed. The cold sweat on her back made her shiver. She pushed down the waistband of her shorts and yanked up the bottom of her t-shirt. The skin around her left hip was even more discoloured than before. A dull grey patch had spread up from the gash and across the bottom of her belly, her veins turning black and prominent. She inserted the tip of the needle into the grey skin, aiming it down the length of one of the veins, and depressed the plunger with her thumb.

The heroin took effect instantly. There was an immediate rush, like she was zooming forward, and then a sudden pullback, like she was sinking into the bed, falling into a world of comforting nothingness. She closed her eyes, nodding off, and as she submerged into the void, the euphoria enveloped her, warmed her, wrapped around her like a powder-blue Snoopy blanket worn to a cottony softness, and the thrumming in her veins whispered, *peace, peace, peace.*

3.

SHE BREATHES PESTILENCE

Cotton.

The high always felt like she was stuffed with cotton, an almost embryonic state where she felt nothing, not the aching of her hip, not even the bed beneath her. Everything around her was dulled and muffled to the point of irrelevance. She hated herself for being a slave to the needle, but she would be lying if she said she didn't still love the high. The warm, drowsy, cottony high. Nothing else mattered when she was high. There was only the initial rush of euphoria and the calm afterglow that gave her an impenetrable sense of safety and warmth. It felt like being loved. She wished it could last forever. But, like love, it never did.

After Drew had walked out on her, she'd fallen into a pit so dark she didn't recognize herself anymore. She left the last scraps of her life behind, bailed on her lease, and used the money from the sale of her parents' house to throw herself madly into the hunt for the Dragon. As far as she was concerned, the old Georgia was dead, and all the hurt had died with her. She didn't have to think about the things left behind if she buried herself in the chase. But the hurt wasn't really dead, it had only gone deep, and it surfaced like a hungry shark whenever Georgia let her guard down.

Her guard had been down in North Carolina, when she met Zack . . .

The visions led her to an out-of-the-way roadhouse tucked deep in the pines and sweetgum, the building already starting to collapse in on itself. Inside, the floor was littered with bones and chunks of meat, but the Dragon was long gone, the trail cold. Frustrated and angry, she drove aimlessly for hours. She thought of her parents murdered and the Dragon still unpunished, chewed her nails and slapped the steering wheel. Finally she stopped the car and collapsed into sobs.

I can't do this, *she thought.* I'm sorry, Dad, I can't! *When the crying waned, she looked up to see she'd stopped before a big bus station somewhere outside Asheville. She went inside to use the restroom, where she cried some more in the stall and hoped no one heard. When she left, she saw a man standing outside the restrooms, hands in his pockets, watching people walk back and forth. He was handsome, a couple of years older than her with a shaggy mop of sandy blond hair, and there was so much hurt in his eyes, such an aura of being lost and alone, that Georgia got the sense she was looking into a mirror. They smiled at each other and started talking. She learned his name was Zack, and by the time the night turned to dawn they were kissing on a bench in a deserted park.*

She leaned against Zack's shoulder and said, "I can't believe this. I barely know you." She shook her head. A chuckle escaped her throat. "How the hell did this happen so fast?"

Zack put his hand under her chin and tipped her head up so he could look at her. "I knew the moment I saw you. I saw it in your eyes. You looked like you'd been crying. You don't have to tell me what happened, that's not my business, but I think we're both in the same place. For me, it's my folks. They're gone. We had a big fight. My mom called me a disappointment, and my old man told me I was dead to him. I guess that leaves me on my own. An orphan."

"Me too," she said. "My parents are gone." She paused, then forced herself to say the word. "Dead."

He nodded, held her a little tighter and said, "I think that's why we were drawn to each other so quickly. We're kindred spirits."

She smirked. "Did you get that from a movie or something? Do you read romance novels?"

"Make fun all you want, you know I'm right. But I've got just the thing. Something that makes life a little more bearable." He unzipped the backpack at his feet and pulled out a rolled up leather pack. He undid the strap, unrolled it and showed her what was inside.

Remembering how Drew had accused her of being on drugs, Georgia laughed so hard Zack drew back with a mix of shame and horror on his face.

"I . . . I'm sorry," he stuttered. "I shouldn't have—"

Georgia snatched the works out of his hands. Anything, she thought, anything to stop feeling like this. *"Show me how," she said.*

Zack smiled with relief. He took her leg and positioned her foot in his lap. He slipped off her shoe and said, "Here, in the webbing between your toes. So no one sees the tracks."

He showed her how to prepare the fix, and the first time the needle hit her vein, she understood what she'd been looking for all along. Something to take the pain away and replace it with heaven. The old mewling, weak Georgia and all her hurt fell back into her coffin and stayed there.

Zack didn't have a home. He was a traveller like her. They drove from state to state in her old car. He asked about the shotgun in the trunk, and when she told him it belonged to her father, he never brought it up again, never asked what her father had needed it for or why she still had it. It was as if he was so grateful to have someone in his life that he didn't want to risk knowing anything bad. They moved anonymously from motel room to motel room, slipping out in the dead of night, leaving their bills unpaid. When they couldn't find motels, they found empty shacks in the woods or old warehouse lofts to crash in. When the heroin ran out, Georgia used her money to buy more. When that ran out, she sold what little jewellery she owned. When there was no more jewellery to sell, she'd offered to hock the shotgun . . .

"No, no way," he said. They were driving on the highway, Zack behind the wheel. Her mind fogged by the afterglow of

a high, she didn't know which highway it was, or even which direction they were heading. All the roads looked the same. Zack's stringy hair poked out from beneath a black wool cap he'd found in a dumpster behind a Burger King. He shook his head vehemently. "The shotgun, the car, they're all you have left of your family. I'm not going to let you lose that. You've done so much already. Too much. Let me take care of you, okay? I don't want you to have to do anything. Let me play knight in shining armour for a while. I know what to do. I've been scoring a lot longer than you."

As the sun went down, they parked and found a crumbling old shack in the woods with nothing inside but a bare, soiled mattress and some empty beer bottles and crumpled cigarette packs covered in a mist of cobwebs and mould. Zack spent the night away while Georgia stayed curled up on the mattress, fiending, chewing her fingernails, twisting her hair into knots. Wondering if he would ever come back. It felt like years passed, but he returned in the early morning, his skin glazed with a fine sheen of sweat, his hair messed up. He looked tired.

"Doctor's got the scrip, babe."

Georgia crawled off the mattress and stared at the bag in his hand. The score was big, more than they'd had in a long time. "Where did you get all this? How could you afford it?"

"I was at the bus station all night, and then the train station, and some guys there knew where to score."

"But how . . . ?"

"Don't worry about it. Get the needle."

But the doses never lasted long enough. Zack disappeared more and more as their need grew, and when the local cops started recognizing him around the bus and train stations they moved on to the next town or the next state. Zack grew distant. Sometimes he wouldn't let her touch him. One night, lying together in a Motel 6 in Charleston, Zack whispered into the dark, *"Do you love me? The things I do for money . . . How can you?"* But she was already nodding off from the high and didn't answer.

She never told him about the Dragon. After what had happened with Drew, she didn't want to risk losing her only friend, and besides, there was no reason to tell him. The Dragon wasn't part of her life anymore. As far as she'd been concerned, the hunt was over. When the Dragon killed and the visions came, she put the needle between her toes and let it take her away.

Georgia's eyes fluttered open in her motel room. She felt sweaty and heavy and only half awake. Part of her was still in the cottony void, still on the road with Zack looking for the next score. The room was dark, and she wondered if the other bedside lamp had burned out too. She didn't remember turning it off. The bathroom door creaked open. She heard the clank of something metallic and heavy hitting the floor, then heard it again. A dark form walked out of the bathroom, each footstep like someone knocking a baseball bat against a pipe. Her eyes struggled to adjust to the dark, but she kept losing focus on the figure. It was a man, that much she knew. A man in an ancient suit of armour so black it seemed to suck the light out of the room. A black helmet covered his head, the visor down over his face.

She wanted to tell him she was sorry. For not having killed the Dragon yet. For being a drug addict. For being weak. She was too drowsy to speak, but she knew nothing she could say would matter anyway. She'd let him down, and his disappointment stung her like a slap in the face.

He reached for his helmet, lifted the visor. There was no face inside, only an infinite blackness. The blackness enveloped her, and within it images appeared.

She saw golden-haired Siegfried, millennia ago, spearing the dragon Fafnir before the mouth of a misty Teutonic cave. Further back in time, she saw Thor, his muscles straining through his skin as he thrashed the Midgard Serpent Jörmungandr against the rugged, rocky fjords of Norway; and further still to Indra, in his colourful Hindu headdress, wrestling with the three-headed serpent Vritra the Enveloper in the jungles of India; and the Hittite storm god Tarhun, bolts of lightning glinting off the edges of his double-bladed axe as he slew the dragon Illuyankas amid the olive groves of Turkey; all the way back to Marduk of Sumer, a titanic shadow against the black emptiness of space, cutting the dragon Tiamat to pieces and creating the world from her bones.

Dragonslayers. The old ones, from long ago. She'd only been seven years old the first time she heard their names . . .

Georgia wandered into the living room, wiping the candy stickiness of her midday snack from her chubby fingers. The afternoon sun through the windows painted a rosy golden glow over her father sitting on the couch. He was reading an old book, its scaly leather binding tattered and falling apart.

"What's that?" Georgia asked. Her father started, so engrossed in reading he hadn't heard her come in. He closed the book quickly, but she climbed onto the couch next to him. "What are you reading, Daddy?"

Her father sighed. "I hadn't planned to show this to you until you were much older."

"Is it bad?"

"No, not exactly. Here, it's okay, take a look." He opened the book again, positioning it so she could see. The first pages were full of woodcut illustrations and reproduced paintings of giant serpents and lizards.

"They look like dragons," Georgia said.

"They are."

Georgia laughed. Her father was being silly. Everyone knew dragons weren't real.

She saw his eyes scan the pages, so she did the same. Next to the illustrations were stanzas of poetry written in languages she didn't recognize. Someone had penciled English translations in the margins beside them in handwriting that looked a lot like her father's. She read along with him, tales of dragons and gods and heroes, but the strange names like Illuyankas and Marduk confused and frustrated her. Her father stroked her hair, and she snuggled against him, the familiar scent of tobacco and aftershave clouding over her.

"It's okay, Georgia," he said. "You'll understand better when you're older. I really should have waited, but . . ." He

shrugged. *"This book will yours someday."*

"It's got a lot of stories in it," Georgia said. *"Too many to read."* Her father laughed at that, and Georgia felt sunshine inside. She liked making him laugh.

"You think it's too much, huh?" he said. *"Well, here's a secret, kiddo. It's all actually the same story. The same story told throughout time, just with different names and in different places. It's a story we're part of now. You and me and Mom."*

He turned the pages until he found what he was looking for—a painting of a man in a black suit of armour and a black helmet sitting astride a rearing horse. A halo burned over the man's helmet, and in his hand was a long lance, its tip buried in the breast of a small, winged dragon dying in the dirt below. Beneath the painting were the words *"Saint George, by Gustave Moreau, 1870–1889."*

"Another dragon?" she moaned, bored. When would her father let her go outside again? The sun was almost down, and then it'd be dinnertime and off to bed before she knew it.

"I need you to pay attention, sweetheart. One day you may need to know all this as well as I do." Her father pointed to the man on the horse. *"That's George of Cappadocia. Saint George, they call him. He's your great-great-great . . . well, I'm not sure how far back it goes, but he's a distant ancestor of ours."*

"Really?" She perked up, interested again. *"That's your name too. George."*

"Yes, it is. And my father's too. And his father's."

"And mine! Georgia is kind of like George."

Her father grinned. "It's a family tradition. And we're a very special family. It was our ancestors, the descendants of Saint George, who put this book together to gather important information in one place. They called it the Book of Ascalon."

"What kind of information?"

"About who we are and what we do."

"What do we do?"

He tapped the picture. "This."

"We kill dragons?"

"Just one," he answered. "There's only one. But the Dragon appears in a new incarnation in every age of history. Reborn over and over. No one knows why or how the Dragon comes back, only that the cycle keeps repeating itself. Dragon and dragonslayer. Over and over, throughout time."

"Why?"

"I don't know, kiddo," he said. "I don't think we're supposed to know. Those names from before, the ones that were hard to pronounce? They were the dragonslayers from long, long ago, and each of them had their own incarnation of the Dragon to fight. They're as much a part of the cycle as I am. As we are."

Georgia frowned, confused. "What does that mean?" It frustrated her that she didn't get it. She liked spending time with her father, especially since he was gone so often. She didn't want to ruin it. She didn't want him to think she was stupid.

CHASING THE DRAGON

"It means the Dragon is out there now and I have to kill her, like the dragonslayers from long ago did. And if I don't, someday, when I'm gone, it'll be up to you. The responsibility usually passes to the oldest son, but we didn't have a son, we had a daughter. You. The first girl dragonslayer."

Her eyes nearly popped out of her head. "Cool!"

Georgia groaned and rolled over on the bed. She wished she could take that moment back, travel through time, shake her younger self by the shoulders and scream in her face, "It's not cool! It's not like a fairy tale!" But still, she remembered that day well, how the excitement had rushed through her when she learned she was different from the other girls at school. Learned she was special.

In the painting, a woman with flowing auburn hair sat watching on the tall rocks behind George and the Dragon. She wore a crown and her hands were clasped in front of her as though she were praying. Georgia thought she looked pretty. "Who's that lady? Is she a princess?"

Her father took a deep breath. "That's what everyone thinks because that's how the story usually goes. Heroes are always rescuing princesses from dragons, aren't they?"

"She isn't a princess?"

"Well, in the legend she's the princess of Cyrene, somewhere in north Africa back in the Fourth Century. The legend goes that the Dragon was causing a famine by eating everything, their crops, their livestock. A strange illness swept the land. They thought the Dragon was poisoning them. They thought they could appease the Dragon with sacrifices so they would be left alone. The princess was

going to be the sacrifice, but George of Cappadocia came to her rescue and killed the Dragon. That's how the legend goes, anyway."

"But that's not what really happened?"

"No."

"Did he kill the Dragon?"

He frowned, deep furrows appearing in his forehead. "Something went wrong. The story was supposed to end there, with the dragonslayer killing the Dragon, just like always, but it didn't. The Dragon survived, escaped, and today, more than a thousand years later, the Dragon is still alive, and the story is still playing out."

"That's stupid. He should've killed it when he had the chance!"

"I agree. It's not supposed to be this way. As long as the Dragon is still here, whatever the plan is, whatever the reason for all the dragons and dragonslayers, is out of whack. Everywhere the Dragon goes, things crumble to dust, like the glue holding everything together has rotted away. The earth cracks. Sinkholes form in the ground. Entropy spreads."

"Enter . . . entra . . ." She stuttered over the word, trying to pronounce it right, but it was already slipping from her mind. "What's that?"

"It's what makes things fall apart. No one knows why, but the longer the Dragon lives, the worse it gets."

She fidgeted, annoyed that he hadn't answered the question she considered the most important of all. "So, Daddy, who's that woman if she's not a princess?"

Georgia's eyes snapped open. Her shorts and t-shirt

were soaked with sweat and stuck to her body. She felt hot, itchy. The windows were still dark. How long had she been nodding off? Minutes? Hours? Time felt bent out of shape. The heroin was still in her veins; she felt it pulling her back down into the void, lulling her to nod off again. Saint George in his black armour was gone from the foot of the bed. In his place stood her father.

"Dad?" He stood silently watching her. She rolled onto her side, unable to look at him. "Why did you have to go? Why did you have to leave me?" She closed her eyes again and drifted into a blackness spotted with flickering lights that looked like tiny candles . . .

"There's one more present," her father said, sliding a giftwrapped box across the kitchen table to her, past the remnants of her birthday cake.

Georgia eyed it suspiciously. "It's not another cardigan like Mom gave me, is it?"

Next to her father, her mother feigned shocked indignation, then said, "If you don't like it, we can exchange it later. I still have receipt."

"Whatever, it's fine," Georgia said, even though there was no way in hell she was going to wear it to school now that she was in Eighth Grade. Not unless she wanted to be completely boy-proof.

She eagerly tore open the present her father had given her. Inside was the Book of Ascalon.

"It's time," her father said. "I told you it would be yours when you got older. You're thirteen now. You're old enough to study it on your own."

"Oh my God!" Georgia's face lit up. "I almost forgot about this!"

Her mother's smile faded from her face. She turned to her husband with an angry glare, then stood up. "Goddamn you, George." He reached for her hand, but she pulled away.

"It's not like we have any choice in the matter," he said softly, but she walked out of the kitchen without another word.

"Is she okay?" Georgia asked.

Her father nodded. "Give her time." He tapped at the book. "I want you study it until you know it all by heart, the way I do, okay? It's important."

She stayed up late that night and read it cover to cover, taking in the true story of George of Cappadocia. It wasn't an illness that plagued Cyrene, not exactly. It was the living dead, bodies rising from their graves to serve the Dragon. In the end, the king of Cyrene presented George with a lance with which to kill the Dragon, a lance coated with an oil milked from the seedpods of an indigenous wildflower. The flower, unnamed in the book, was the only thing in all the kingdom that the Dragon wouldn't devour, and they believed its oil could kill the creature. But the plan failed and George was killed in the battle. The Dragon fled into the countryside with George's firstborn son in pursuit.

She read on and discovered pages that logged the movements of the Dragon over the centuries. In the back were chapters that spoke of a spiritual link between the Dragon and dragonslayer that caused visions whenever she killed, and how to use those visions to track her. The last *page contained a list of seven warnings about the Dragon that had been written so long ago no one knew which of Saint George's descendants had included them.*

> *SHE SPEAKS THROUGH THE DEAD*
> *SHE TAKES EVERYTHING YOU LOVE*
> *SHE BREATHES PESTILENCE*
> *SHE HIDES IN PLAIN SIGHT*
> *SHE IS RULED BY HER APPETITE*
> *THE EARTH CRUMBLES WHERE SHE TREADS*
> *SHE WILL DEVOUR THE WORLD*

The words swirled around her like a vapour in the motel room. *She breathes pestilence.* Georgia thought of the plague of walking dead in Cyrene, and she thought about the gash in her hip, how the grey skin spread out every night from where the Dragon's claws had mauled her. Pestilence. Infection . . .

Her father held up a broom by the handle, its bristles sweeping in the air. "You can't let her claws cut you," he said. "She gets inside you that way. It's like an infection. It'll kill you, and if she's inside you she'll control your body even after you're dead." He shook the broom. "This is her claw. Don't let it touch you."

He chased her around the living room, Georgia nimbly dodging the broom's touch. Her mother sat at the coffee table, pulling a new porcelain angel for her collection from its shipping box. Georgia accidentally knocked the table, and her mother yelled at them to take it outside before they broke something.

They resumed the chase in the back yard. Georgia couldn't help laughing and shrieking as her father tried to hit her with the broom. Each squeal made her father angrier. His face grew beet red. He yelled at her to stop horsing around. He ran faster, smacked the broom across her back, hard enough to hurt, and knocked her onto grass. She lay there, stunned and frightened while he bent over her and pinned her to the ground. "Goddamn it, this isn't a game!" he yelled. "She will kill you! Do you get that, Georgia? She will kill you!"

Georgia stuttered awake in her motel room. Her father stood over her, bending until his face was close to hers.

"Dad, don't go."

"She's killing again," her dead father said.

The vision slammed through her without warning, knocking her back and turning the room red. She convulsed on the bed, her arms flailing, her legs kicking. She saw the screaming faces of men in black bandanas. She saw bodies torn apart by long, sharp claws, and blood, so much blood. She caught a glimpse of a bare concrete wall with the word *Inkhedz* spraypainted across it in choppy, angular letters. She saw an ocean of red flowing across the floor and pooling around the base of a big wooden box, the words *Bristleman Corp., Buckshot Hill, N.M.* stencilled across its slats.

Georgia thrashed on the bed with the needle still half-stuck in her hip. From the corner of her eye, through the blood-soaked vision, she saw her father shake his head and turn away in shame.

4.

SHE HIDES IN PLAIN SIGHT

If the high felt like cotton, coming down was like crashing into the sidewalk after a long fall off a skyscraper. She felt groggy, sore, half dead. The bedspread under her was rumpled and stained with sweat. The sunlight streaming through the translucent motel curtains hurt her eyes. It felt like someone was working a jackhammer against the inside of her skull. She rolled onto her side and sucked in a breath as the needle twisted and popped out of her skin. She looked down at her hip. The flesh had returned to its normal shade of pink, only slightly red around the edges where the needle had stayed stuck in her all night. The grey, infected skin was gone.

She sat up slowly. As she put the needle back in the leather pack, her heart jumped. The small plastic baggie was missing. She crawled to the edge of the bed. Below, the bag sat open where it had fallen, the last of her heroin scattered in a brown powder on the threadbare carpet. She must have knocked it off the bed while in the throes of the vision.

"No, no, no . . ." She tumbled off the bed and tried to scoop it up into the baggie, but all she managed to do was rub it deeper into the filthy fibres of the carpet. She grabbed a tissue from the bathroom and managed to pick up most of the powder with it, but when she looked at what little she'd collected, her heart sank. It was so contaminated with hairs, dust, dirt and bug droppings she'd never be able to separate out anything usable. Cursing, she brought the tissue and its contents into the bathroom and lifted the toilet cover. But as she stood over the bowl, her fingers stubbornly refused to drop it in. Was there enough heroin in the mess for one more high? Trembling, she stared at the filthy powder in the tissue. Brought it closer to her face. Sniffed at it. It didn't have a scent beyond the bitter hint of dust. What if she couldn't find anymore? What if this was it? The thought terrified her. She couldn't let it go to waste. She brought the tissue under her nose. Closed her eyes.

She thought of her father, struck by a vague memory that she'd seen him last night. He'd only been a dream image from her dosed-up mind, but his disappointment had felt so real. What would he think if he were still alive, if he saw her now, standing over the toilet with a tissue full of heroin scooped off the filthy motel carpet? It shamed her, but her body didn't care. Her body buzzed in ecstatic anticipation, urging her onward.

She tentatively put her nose into the tissue and tried to snort it. She wasn't used to snorting. The gritty powder burned her nostrils and triggered a sneezing fit. She managed just enough of a taste to give her a fleeting moment of warmth, followed by an instant craving for more. She wiped her nose, dropped the tissue in the toilet and flushed it.

She watched it swirl and disappear down the drain. She would have to score more, and soon.

Georgia dressed and left the motel room. She brought her works along in her purse. The Buckshot Motor Inn didn't look like the kind of place to have housekeeping service, but just in case, she didn't want anyone to find the needle in her room. Outside, it was already hot and sticky in the morning sun. The parking spot in front of Marcus's room was empty. She remembered him mentioning something about taking his son to a rodeo and breathed a sigh of relief. He'd seen her at her worst last night, jonesing like a fiend. The embarrassment of facing him again would be too much.

She started walking to her car when someone called, "Good morning, miss!" Shading her eyes against the sun, she saw a squat, overweight man with a mess of greying hair on the porch. He was moving a broom back and forth noncommittally in dungarees and a Brooks & Dunn t-shirt that had long sweat stains under the armpits. He leaned the broom against the wall and walked toward her. The rubber soles of his sneakers squeaked annoyingly with each step.

"Morning," she said. She hoped that whatever he wanted, the conversation would be quick. She didn't have time for this.

"Roy Dalton's the name," he said when he reached her. He sounded out of breath and something rattled in the back of his throat. "Owner and operator of this fine establishment." His giant, meaty hand engulfed hers as he shook it. His palm was sweaty and callused. "Just wanted to make sure everything's all right with your room. My boy, Wilbur, he's been working the office for a while now, but he's still young; he forgets things." He coughed and cleared his throat. "He doesn't have that attention to detail you need in the hospitality industry."

"Everything's fine, thanks." She opened the car door.

"Good, good," Roy Dalton said. He cleared his throat again. It was obvious he had more to say. Georgia waited by the open car door. She wished she could just ignore him, get in and take off, but it wasn't a good idea. That kind of rudeness would be remembered. It was better, she knew, to be pleasant and forgettable. "We don't get many visitors in Buckshot Hill, especially single gals like yourself," he continued. "Anyways, with the missus away visiting friends up in Santa Fe, I've got a lot of free time on my hands, so if you need anything, anything at all, you just let ol' Roy know, okay? I aim to please." He smiled, and she saw several of his upper teeth were gone on one side of his mouth, the bottom teeth mashing up against the empty gums.

The missing teeth made her think uncomfortably of entropy. She forced a quick, thin smile, lowered herself into the driver's seat and closed the door. Roy Dalton leaned into the open window on his elbow. A fat droplet of sweat rolled down his arm. She could sense him trying to peek down the neck of her t-shirt. "Hold up a moment," he said.

Georgia sighed, her key halfway to the ignition. Now what?

He wiped his forehead. "You got a look about you, miss, if you don't mind me saying. One I've seen enough to recognize by now. Bags under the eyes, jitters. You looking to score?"

Shit.

Rattled, Georgia feigned righteous indignation. "Excuse me?"

Pathetic. Everything about her voice sounded like a lie.

"It's all right if you are. I ain't judging. I'm just saying I can help you out."

"I don't know what you're talking about." She put her key in the ignition.

"Got a brother who likes a taste of the hard stuff now and then," Roy said. "He wears that same look you got now when the jones comes over him. I know where he gets it, if you're interested."

Georgia didn't say anything, didn't look at him, but she didn't turn the key either.

"Thought as much. See now, what'd I say? Customer service is all about attention to detail. You got nothing to fear from me. I ain't gonna turn you in. I'll tell you where to go, who to ask for, even. I'll make it easy as pie, and all you gotta do in return is give ol' Roy some attention. Show him some gratitude. That doesn't sound so bad, does it?" He grinned and licked his lips.

Georgia felt sick. For a moment she thought of sweet, shy Wilbur, so awkward around girls. The boy would grow up to be just like his father, she realized, and that made her angry. She revved the engine. Roy backed away from the window and waved with a big, fake smile like he wasn't some scumbag looking for a little junkie tail while his wife was away.

She pulled her car out of the parking space, hoping she might accidentally run over his foot, then left the motel lot and drove back into town.

Without Roy's help, though, she didn't know where to go, so she drove through Buckshot Hill with her eyes peeled. She'd been scoring long enough to know what to look for. Cornerboys with shifty glances, cars parked together in groups for no discernable reason, lone musclemen standing guard outside unmarked doors. But after half an hour she still didn't see any of the telltale signs and began to wonder if the town was dry.

No, it couldn't be. Roy had said his brother scored in Buckshot Hill. She just had to look harder. But time was running out. The Dragon could already be on the move. If she lost the Dragon now, there was no telling how long it would be before she picked up the trail again. She didn't have time to wander aimlessly.

She thought of the vision, her dream-father's words—*She's killing again*—and the sight of all those screaming faces. The Dragon had struck again sooner than expected. The crate she'd seen in her vision had been from a company called Bristleman Corp. in Buckshot Hill. But that didn't make sense. The Dragon never struck twice in the same place. It was how she stayed off the radar. Why change that now?

CHASING THE DRAGON

First things first, she thought, trying to clear the jumble in her head. The heroin took priority. Without it . . . she didn't even want to think about what would happen without it. Then, she promised herself, *then* she'd go after the Dragon.

There was still no sign of a dealer. Was she going to have to go back to Roy and take him up on his offer? Jesus. Even Zack had never asked her to trick, though in the darkest days of her addiction she probably would've been willing. But now? The thought of Roy Dalton's hands on her, his half-toothless mouth, repulsed her.

There was one more place she could look. She turned the car in the right direction as best she could remember and passed through the small downtown area. The tables in front of the ice cream parlour were empty now. Bits of trash blew and tumbled in the breeze where the young couples had sat. It filled her with a sudden and inexplicable sadness. She kept driving, past the quiet little houses, abandoned now for work and school. A few minutes later she found herself back in the warehouse district. Her last, best chance.

She slowed as she drove past the wide, boxy buildings. Boards were nailed across the doors and windows, the walls spray-painted with everything from simple tags to a block-long mural of a lasso-spinning cowboy on a winged horse. Someone had sprayed what looked like a Chinese character on the horse's rear end.

Unsure of where to go, Georgia drove up and down the streets between the warehouses, looking for any sign of drug activity. She didn't see anything. She felt itchy. She thought of the screaming faces from her visions, of the Dragon getting away and killing more people, of Roy Dalton's hands all over her, and she started to panic.

Rounding a corner, she spotted someone walking at the end of the block and slowed the car. It was the hobo she'd seen last night, swinging the same Dunkin Donuts coffee cup in his hand. She tailed him, driving slowly and staying far back so she wouldn't spook him. She followed him for three more blocks until he came to a warehouse with yellow cement walls and boarded windows. She stopped the car and watched. The hobo tapped on a metal door at the corner of the building. It opened a moment later, and a kid who looked like he couldn't have been older than thirteen stepped out onto the sidewalk. His skin was pale white, as if he didn't spend much time outside. His skinny body swam inside an oversized Lobos basketball jersey. Gold chains hung around his neck. He wore a yellow bandana on his head, his eyes hidden behind sunglasses that were too big for his face. When he spoke, something in his mouth gleamed in the sunlight.

The hobo tipped the coffee cup into his hand and passed the pile of coins over to the boy. The boy counted them and stuffed them in his pocket. He disappeared into the warehouse for a moment. When the boy came out again, he shook the hobo's hand, and Georgia smirked. It was an old dealer's trick. Shake hands and slip the package into the buyer's palm, in case you were being watched.

After the hobo left, Georgia got out of the car and walked toward the warehouse, her purse slung over her shoulder. The boy saw her coming and glanced back at the door nervously, but he didn't bolt. Instead, he nodded at her and said, "'Sup, girl?" He smiled, and the sunlight reflected off a gold-plated grill across his front teeth.

"You holding?" she asked.

Blue eyes peered at her over the top of his sunglasses. "Who's askin'?"

"I'm not a cop," she said.

He laughed. "Girl, please. Everyone knows ain't no cops in Buckshot. Nearest we got is the State Troopers out past the exit ramp, and they don't give a shit what we do. Only time I ever see 'em is when rich folks get hurt." He looked her up and down and said, "So what you lookin' for, girl? I got whatever you need. Pot. Meth. Coke. You scorin' for your boyfriend? You got a boyfriend?"

"Horse," she said.

"Horse! Now *that's* what I'm talkin' about!" he shouted, punching the air. "Girl likes to *party*!" She noticed a Chinese character tattooed on his shoulder, the same symbol she'd seen on the cowboy mural. A gang tag.

"So do you have it?"

He nodded, stroking the peach fuzz on his chin. "Yeah, I can get it for you, no sweat."

She felt the last of her panic drain away, replaced by a jittery anticipation. "How fast?"

"Pssshhhhh, two shakes. It's right inside. Gram'll cost you two."

"Two *hundred*?"

"Hells yeah, girl. There a problem?"

"That's twice what I normally pay."

The kid sucked his teeth. "What can I say? Times

ain't normal. There's been a market adjustment. Ain't no competition anymore. We can charge whatever we want. Take it or leave it."

She opened her wallet. Her parents' faces swam up to meet her from the photograph inside, judging her with their silent smiles. Georgia avoided their eyes and did a quick count of the bills she'd taken from the diner. The two hundred dollar price tag would clean her out.

"We're the Shaolin Tong," the white kid said, puffing up his skinny chest proudly. "Our shit's the best there is, girl. Worth every penny, trust me. They call me Egg Foo, and I'm big around here, real important, you feel me? Ask anyone. I wouldn't steer you wrong. So, you want that gram of horse or what?"

Sighing, she handed him the money. She didn't have a choice. The clock was ticking. Egg Foo counted them, then stuffed them into his jeans pocket.

"Wait here," he said. "Like I said, two shakes."

Egg Foo disappeared inside, closing the door behind him, but it banged against the jamb and instead of latching properly it swung open again. A single bulb hung from the ceiling just inside the doorway. A lone brown moth fluttered and tinked against it until wisps of smoke rose from its wings. Cool air wafted toward her on the low hum of an air conditioner. In the distance, she saw Egg Foo strutting toward a door in the far wall with the chipped remains of the word MANAGER stencilled on the frosted glass. From where she stood, it looked like it said ANGER. Egg Foo appeared tiny from behind, just a skinny little kid in an oversized jersey, and suddenly she got the joke of his name: Egg Foo, as in young.

A moment after the boy disappeared behind the door, a large blonde woman stepped into Georgia's field of vision. She was squeezed into a black tube top several sizes too small, her belly drooping over her belt like the top of a muffin. In her hand was an enormous Slurpee cup. The same Chinese character was tattooed on her wrist.

"Are you here to kill us?" she asked. Though she looked to be in her late thirties, her voice was that of a child, high-pitched and innocent, but also lazy, as if it took too much effort to pronounce every word. Bright red lipstick stood out against her pale, pasty skin. Apparently there were no actual Asians in the Shaolin Tong.

"No," Georgia replied. "I'm not here to kill anyone."

The woman smiled around the straw of her Slurpee. "Then you can be my friend. Come in out of the sun."

She stepped inside and closed the door behind her. Immediately the air conditioning enveloped her, and Georgia, grateful to be out of the heat, felt the sweat drying on her body.

The woman beckoned for her to follow, leading her across the bare cement floor of a large room. The cinderblock walls were covered with posters of old kung fu movies, *Five Deadly Venoms*, *The Kid with the Golden Arm*, *The 36th Chamber of Shaolin*, *Drunken Master*. A poster for *Enter the Dragon* was tacked up over a window, the sunlight shining through and making Bruce Lee glow like he was radioactive. An ash-stained pool table stood in the middle of the room. The floor was littered with cigarette butts and old pizza boxes. Empty bottles of Jack Daniels and Crazy Horse cluttered the corners.

The woman stopped in front of a door decorated with glittery stickers of rainbows and stars. "This is my room," she said.

Up close her eyes looked unfocused, dreamy, and Georgia realized she was high. The woman swung open the door, took Georgia by the hand and pulled her inside. A plush blue carpet ran the length of the floor, and two standing lamps in opposite corners painted the ceiling red and green with their coloured bulbs. An aquarium tank atop a small table glowed blue from an internal light, turning the fish into dark silhouettes that swam in lazy circles. A glass crack pipe lay next to it, its stem marked with the same garish red as her lipstick.

The woman went to the window at the far end of the room, where the boards nailed to the outside cut the sunlight into strips. "I like my room because it has a window and I can look outside. I don't get to go out very often." She turned away from Georgia, and her tone became quiet, confidential. "I saw shapes out there last night. I thought it was the Inkheads. Sometimes they try to rob us. But that wasn't it. Whoever it was kept moving."

Georgia stiffened. Inkheads. She'd seen that name in the vision: *Inkhedz* scrawled on a wall during the Dragon's attack. The screaming faces. "Tell me about the Inkheads," she said.

The woman shrugged. "They're gone." She spread her fingers to emulate a cloud of smoke. "Poof. Just like that. Some pothead came by this morning, said he used to buy from them but had to come to us instead. He said there was blood everywhere."

Georgia chewed her lip. So the Dragon hadn't left Buckshot Hill after all. But why go after the Inkheads? The Dragon's hunger was insatiable; she would eat everything in her path, given the opportunity. But she'd managed to control herself before, normally moving on for hundreds of miles before feeding again. What had kept her in Buckshot Hill? What could possibly be of interest to her here?

"Did you see anything else? What did the shapes look like?"

The woman shrugged and said, "Do you like my fish?" Her eyes followed the fish swimming laps around the glowing blue tank.

"This is important," Georgia said. "What did you see?"

The blonde woman pouted. "Nothing, all right? Nothing. I'm no snitch." She brushed by Georgia to put her Slurpee on the table. Up close, she smelled of bitter smoke, sweat and cheap shampoo. "I heard you with Egg Foo outside," the woman said. "You're chasing the dragon."

Georgia's heart pushed into her throat. "What did you say?"

"Isn't that what they call it? Heroin?" She picked up the crack pipe and fished a lighter out of her pocket. "You want a hit?"

"No, what I want is for you to tell me what you saw. Which way did the shapes go?"

The woman laughed. "Whatever. Suit yourself. I can't keep away from this stuff. You know what it's like. Sometimes you chase the dragon, and sometimes the dragon chases you, right?" She lit the pipe and took a long drag. A cloud of smoke seeped from her mouth, and then her face slackened and her eyes glazed over as the drug took hold.

"Which way did they go?" Georgia pressed.

The woman looked up at the coloured lights playing along the ceiling. "Sometimes I think I can see heaven up there."

Frustrated, Georgia turned away. In the quiet of the woman's room, she felt how hard she'd crashed—harder than she thought. Her headache was still there, buzzing just under the surface. She felt itchy again and only then realized she'd been scratching her arm without knowing it. Her stomach was twisted in knots. Somehow, watching the fish swim back and forth helped. It was calming. Serene. Another fix would help too. Just a small one, enough to get her in fighting shape to go after the Dragon. She could go right back to the motel and have a little taste.

No, there was no time for that. She couldn't let the Dragon slip away again. She wished Egg Foo would hurry up.

"I could watch them all day," the blonde woman whispered next to her. "They don't care that they're not getting anywhere. They just keep swimming."

Georgia watched the fish glide in the deep blue light. *Stainless*, she thought, and she tried to put it from her mind but the rest kept coming, *Stainless Steel Stanley's* and *"Found you, child,"* and she fought against it but the fish were swimming back and forth like a hypnotist's watch, and then the memory broke through and she couldn't stop it from unspooling . . .

In the empty parking lot behind a closed convenience store, Georgia sank down in a nest of candy wrappers and crushed soda cans, her back against the wall and her pockets filled with the change she'd begged off people on the rich side of town. She thought of Zack out scoring somewhere. She was supposed to meet him soon, back at the old, decrepit hunting cabin they'd been sleeping in, but she couldn't keep her eyes open. She tried to focus on the billboard that rose high over the woods behind the parking lot. STAINLESS STEEL STANLEY'S, it said, RESTAURANT SUPPLY, EXIT 9. There was a big picture of a fish laid out on a wide steel spatula, sliced open down the middle and stuffed with lemons, its head still attached, its beady black eyes staring back at her. Disgusting. She closed her eyes so she wouldn't have to look at it. Nodded off.

When she opened her eyes again, it was getting dark and a man was standing over her, his sickly grey skin marbled with black veins. Half his face had been shorn from his skull. In his hand was a blood-edged straight razor. "Found you, child," the meat puppet said.

Behind it, twigs and branches snapped as a dark shape moved through the woods toward her. The Dragon.

Georgia struggled groggily to her feet, turned to run, but the meat puppet grabbed her. It slammed her face-first against the wall and held her there.

The hand pressing her face to the wall pulled away and was immediately replaced by another. Scaly and hard. Long ivory claws closed over the top of her head.

"You hid yourself well, child," the Dragon said. "But you must have known you could not hide forever. You knew I would come eventually. It is our nature to be bound together.

But I give you credit. You were not where I thought to find you. Someone else was. A clever ruse. One that shall be properly punished with agony."

"I don't know what you mean," Georgia sobbed. "What ruse? I didn't do anything!"

A second claw appeared from behind her, sliding around to her belly. The long talons scratched lightly through her shirt—not hard enough to draw blood, just enough to let her know they were there. "I wonder what you will taste like." The Dragon sniffed her. "Dirt, perhaps. Desperation and filth and need. Very different from your father."

Tears spilled down Georgia's face. Panic kept her from catching her breath. "You don't have to do this. It's over. The whole thing is over. I don't care anymore. That's why I stopped coming after you. We can just leave each other alone now. You can go do whatever you want. I don't care. We never have to see each other again. Just go!"

Hot breath hit the back of Georgia's head. The Dragon was laughing. "And never taste your flesh? Never experience the joy of watching you die? No, I think not, child."

The Dragon's claw tightened against her belly. Georgia thought of herself on a giant spatula, her stomach slit open, filled with lemons. Dead black eyes. "I have looked far and wide for you, child. I have earned my reward."

Georgia spasmed in fear, her body twisted, and instead of slashing open her stomach, the claw tore through her jeans and the flesh beneath, practically down to the bone of her hip. Georgia watched her own blood spill out of her body like juice from a carton, saw shreds of her own skin stuck in the fibres of her torn jeans, and she started hyperventilating. The world buckled and darkened at the edges.

As unconsciousness enveloped her, she thought she heard a piercing, inhuman scream. Thought she saw the Dragon run back into the woods and the meat puppet stumble aimlessly like a marionette with cut stings. Then the world went away.

Later, she woke up in the pitch black night. Bleeding and weak, Georgia crawled through the woods toward the hunting cabin. Crawled home to Zack. She found him curled on the floor in a pool of blood. He had cuts all over his hands, defensive wounds, and one big cut across his throat. The kind a straight razor might make. The Dragon had come to the cabin looking for her, Georgia realized, and found Zack instead.

The rolled-up leather pack was still where he left it on the bed. Inside was the full bag of heroin he'd scored. The skin around her wound was already turning grey from the Dragon's infection. She didn't have much time. Sobbing, she curled up next to Zack's body. Too weak to reach her toes or even break the skin, she injected the drug directly into the open, bleeding wound in her hip. One final high as the Dragon's infection unfolded inside her. She wondered if it would hurt to die, and if being high would make it hurt less. She wondered if the Dragon would turn her into a meat puppet, and if she'd know, if she'd be trapped and helpless in the shell of her corpse. Then the heroin knocked her out and threw her into a black void from which she knew she would never return.

But she did. Hours later, she woke up clutching Zack's cold, stiff hand, very much surprised to be alive. The wound had stopped bleeding. The grey, infected skin was gone.

Somehow the heroin had kept the infection at bay. She didn't know why, and frankly she didn't care as long it kept working.

The infection tried to spread again the next night, and the night after that, and each time she fought it back with the heroin. The infection never cleared up; it lived inside her where the Dragon had mauled her, but the drug dammed its flow through her system, stopped it from killing her and giving the Dragon control of her body.

Somehow, with an irony so absurd it felt like a bad joke, her worst, most self-destructive habit had become the only thing keeping her alive.

She buried Zack in a shallow grave in the woods and holed up in the cabin for months, leaving only to beg for change to score more heroin and, occasionally, to eat.

Finally, when she was strong enough, when the wound was healing well and she had a handle on the infection, she loaded up the car. Then she brought a wildflower to Zack's grave.

"I'm going now," she told the dirt. "I'm going after her. It's what I should have been doing all this time. If I'd done what I was supposed to . . ." Her chin quivered. She bit her lip. "None of this would have happened. It's all my fault. I'm going to find her." She dropped the flower on his grave. "I'm going to make her pay."

"Hey!" The angry shout ripped Georgia out of her

memories. Egg Foo stood in the doorway of the blonde woman's room. He stalked inside and slapped the woman upside the head. Georgia winced at the sharp sound, but the woman didn't even seem to notice. "The fuck is she doing in here? Huh? The fuck's the matter with you, you fucking cow? No one comes inside! You got that? No one!"

He grabbed the woman's arm and shook her, but she only giggled. She looked at Georgia with her cloudy, doped eyes and said, "She's glowing. See? So pretty. Glowing like an angel."

Egg Foo pushed her back. "Bitch is fucked up. You," he said to Georgia, "let's go." He led her out of the room and back toward the front door. He stuck a small zip-locked baggie in her hand.

"Thanks."

He didn't answer. He opened the door and they both walked out onto the sidewalk.

"Is it true about the Inkheads?" she asked. "They're all dead? No survivors at all?"

"Yo, fuck 'em," Egg Foo said. "They got what they deserved, trash-talkin' motherfuckers. Their shit wasn't no good, neither. That's why they kept trying to steal ours. Probably a pissed off customer that took 'em out. People died smoking the Inkheads' rock, and that shit's bad for business, you feel me? But whoever wasted 'em last night did us a big favour. Now we *own* this backass town."

"Where did the Inkheads hang out?"

"The fuck you care, bitch? You got your horse, now ride it the fuck outta here." He sucked his teeth at her, then went back inside and slammed the door. It stayed closed this time.

Walking the long stretch of sidewalk back to her car, Georgia unrolled the leather pack, dropped the baggie inside, and put it all back in her purse. She opened the car door, the sun-heated handle stinging her fingers, and lowered herself into the steaming heat of the vehicle. She drove off slowly, checking the buildings as she passed.

She found what she was looking for on the other side of the warehouse district: a corroded, run-down box of a building with a big name painted across the front windows: BRISTLEMAN CORP.

She parked across the street, grabbed the shotgun out of the back seat and walked carefully toward the building. No yellow tape criss-crossed the doorway, no officers guarded the crime scene—Egg Foo hadn't lied about the police not caring what happened in Buckshot Hill. The front door was unlocked. She nudged it open with the shotgun and stepped through. It was dark inside, and unlike the Shaolin Tong's air-conditioned warehouse, the air here was stifling. Her purse, still slung over her shoulder, banged against her side. Cursing, she dropped it to the floor. She should have left it in the car. Stupid of her.

Get it together, girl, she thought.

She took another step, and her shoe landed in something slick. Blood. The floor was drenched with it, pooling around the overturned metal tables, the chairs scattered across the room, the dusty wooden crates piled in the corners. Red arcs spattered the walls, half-obliterating the word *Inkhedz* spraypainted across one of them. Playing cards were stuck in the puddles of blood. The Inkheads must have been surprised in the middle of a game. She peeled a card off the bottom of her shoe—King of Hearts, the suicide king, with his sword up against his head. His face was smeared with blood like he was bleeding from his own self-inflicted wound. She let it fall to the floor.

She didn't see any bodies. Blood, an ocean of it, but no bodies, not even any bones or meat left behind. If the Dragon hadn't eaten them, what had she done with them?

A door at the far end of the warehouse burst open, startling her. Shapes lumbered out of the shadows. The shafts of light from the front windows fell first on the black bandanas on their heads, then on their grey, black-veined skin, their blood-soaked sleeveless t-shirts and baggy shorts.

She pumped a shell into the shotgun chamber, one of the three remaining shells still in the tube running under the barrel, and realized then that she'd forgotten to reload after the fight at the diner. Her father had trained her better than that. She'd gotten sloppy.

Only three shots. She scanned the dead Inkheads lurching toward her and counted eight of them. Her stomach filled with ice.

"She will kill you! Do you get that, Georgia? She will kill you!"

In her mind, she saw the box of shotgun shells sitting uselessly by her suitcase in the motel room.

5.

SHE IS RULED BY HER APPETITE

Georgia backed toward the warehouse exit, but one look at the dead hands groping for her from the shadows told her she wouldn't make it. The meat puppets had moved too close. Even with their slow, clumsy movements, she knew they'd trap her in the narrow doorway before she could escape. She didn't have a choice—she stepped to the side, trying to circle around them, and trying to keep enough distance from the wall behind her so she wouldn't get pinned. The meat puppets turned in unison, following her with their lifeless eyes.

"Where are you?" she called. "Stop hiding and show yourself, you coward!" Her voice shook, and she hated herself for it. It made her sound like a scared little girl. With her hands trembling around the shotgun, she wondered if maybe that was all she really was.

CHASING THE DRAGON

The Dragon laughed, the sound echoing out of eight different mouths. One meat puppet stepped forward, away from the others. Its black Inkheads bandana was soaked with blood, and a long red gash stretched from its neck to its chest.

It leapt toward her. She glimpsed the other seven behind it shift position suddenly, but she didn't have time to see what they were doing. She raised the shotgun and squeezed the trigger. The meat puppet's head exploded in red and white fragments, and the echo of the report slammed off the warehouse walls like thunder. The body dropped to the floor and stayed there.

One, she thought. She pumped the shotgun, and the spent shell clattered to the floor. Only two left. She had to make them count or she'd die in this place.

She turned to the others, and her chest tightened when she realized what had happened. The one she'd shot had been a distraction, sacrificed so the others would have time to reach into the back of their waistbands and pull their guns. Now they stood in front of her with automatic pistols in their fists, their cracked, dead lips curling into smug sneers.

Georgia willed her legs to move. She ran for the door. A spot on the floor in front of her exploded suddenly. Cement chips flew into the air. She skidded to a stop. Smoke wafted from the barrel of the nearest meat puppet's gun.

Georgia backed away from the doorway. The Dragon was toying with her. She wasn't going to let Georgia get away that easily. The other meat puppets raised their guns.

She started running a moment before the shots rang

out, pumping her legs like mad and diving behind one of the overturned metal tables. She crouched low against the sticky, blood-slick floor. The table jerked toward her, the metal puckering with each thudding impact of the bullets. How long could the table hold up under the attack? How long until the bullets broke though?

The echo of gunshots died, replaced with an eerie quiet. She rose to her knees and peered around the corner of the table. The meat puppets lurched toward her.

Georgia swung the shotgun up, aiming over the top of the table, and squeezed off a shot. It hit one of them in the face, sprinkling the air with blood and brain matter. It dropped to its knees, then fell flat.

Two.

She crouched behind the table again. The six remaining meat puppets squeezed off shots, but their dead hands were too clumsy and the bullets went wide, punching holes in the wall behind her. Plaster dust rained down on her hair. She risked another peek and saw them spreading out, three moving to her left, the other three to her right, trying to encircle her.

They outnumbered her, but they were slow and ungainly. That gave her a slight advantage. Her *only* advantage. If she was going to make it out of there alive, she had to keep moving.

Another metal table lay on its side just a few feet away. She hugged the shotgun tight to her side and leapt for it. A bullet whizzed beneath her, digging into the floor. She landed badly behind it, skidding in a pool of blood. Her knee banged against the hard cement floor. Her elbows felt skinned, but with so much blood on the floor, her clothes, her skin, it was hard to tell if any of it was hers. More shots rang out, and flecks of metal chipped off the top edge of the table. Georgia flinched, ducking.

"I grow tired of this game," the Dragon said through their mouths. She sounded angry, frustrated.

Sweat dripped from Georgia's hair and rolled down her neck. The pain in her knee was sharp and getting worse. She wondered if she'd fractured the bone. The odds of making it out of there with a bum leg and only one shot left weren't good.

"Your father played a similar game with me, child."

Georgia froze. Her throat tightened.

"He was a good warrior, put up a grand battle, until I slit him open from his throat to his belly and feasted on his organs. And your mother, oh how she wailed and beat me with her fists. When I devoured her, she tasted like tears."

Georgia wanted to cover her ears, but she didn't dare let go of the shotgun. She wished the Dragon would shut up. She wanted to *make* the Dragon shut up. She hated that voice. Hated the way it made her feel small and powerless. Hated the things it made her remember. The late night phone call from the police, speeding from her and Drew's apartment to her parents' house with her heart in her throat . . .

"Miss Quincey, don't," the police officer said, trying to restrain her at the front door.

She struggled against him. "Let me through! I'm their daughter!"

"You don't want to see this," the officer said. "Trust me."

"Let her in," someone called from inside.

The officer let her pass, and she discovered the man who had spoken was a police detective in a rumpled suit. He met her in the entrance hallway and introduced himself, but his name passed unregistered through her frightened, anxious mind. She couldn't look the detective in the eye, kept looking at his throat instead, the spots of stubble on his Adam's apple. There was a faded red mark where he must have cut himself shaving that morning. He turned and led her into the house.

The first thing she noticed was a bloodstain seeping into the living room carpet. The same carpet where she'd played with her dolls when she was little. The couch where she'd sat when her father first showed her the Book of Ascalon was shredded, thick white upholstery clouding out of the gashes. The picture window was shattered, furniture overturned. The shelving units along the walls were broken, and beneath them lay blood-spattered piles of books and picture frames. The shattered remains of the porcelain angels her mother had spent a lifetime collecting.

The Dragon. She must have followed Georgia's father home and caught him by surprise. Georgia didn't see the shotgun anywhere, no holes in the walls or shells on the floor, no gunpowder tang in the air. Her father hadn't even had time to get the shotgun from where he kept it in the trunk of his car.

The detective led her toward her parents' bedroom at the back of the house. The door was gone, smashed to splinters.

"I don't know if you're up for it," he said, "but time is of the essence if we're going to catch who did this. We need your help making a positive identification."

Georgia stepped through the doorway and immediately turned away from the glistening, red, lifeless things scattered along the floor. She'd glimpsed hair, a wristwatch at the stump of a hand. She felt her gorge rising.

"There isn't much to go on," the detective said.

"It's them."

"You're sure? These are your parents, George and Tanya Quincey?"

She nodded. They must have barricaded themselves in the bedroom as a last resort. It hadn't stopped the Dragon for long.

Georgia lost it then, vomiting in the corner of the room.

When she was done, the detective said, "I'm very sorry for your loss, Miss Quincey. Do you have any idea who would do this to your parents?"

She shook her head and hid her face behind her hands.

"This is overkill for your typical robbery gone bad. Usually when we see this level of violence, it's personal. Was anyone angry at them? Did they have any enemies you know of?"

"No," she lied. "No enemies."

He nodded and gave a strange little grunt. "You ever seen anything like this before?"

She shook her head.

He grunted again. "Okay. We found multiple footprints on the carpet. At least three separate pairs of shoes, not to mention one set we can't even be sure are footprints at all. You wouldn't know anything about that, would you?"

"No."

"If we run those prints, are you sure they're not going to come back to someone you know, someone you're not telling me about? Maybe an ex-boyfriend with a grudge? Or maybe someone who's not an ex but knows an only child stands to clear a hefty sum from life insurance?"

She glared at him. "You think I had something to do with this?"

He grunted again, and she realized it was the sound he made when he was sceptical about something. "I don't know anything yet, Miss Quincey. Only that things aren't adding up. Like how come there's no murder weapon? How come it looks like a wild animal got at them? But most of all, Miss Quincey, I couldn't help noticing that you may look upset, but you don't look at all surprised."

"I don't know what to tell you." She felt cold and hugged herself.

He slipped her his business card. "If you think of anything that might help the investigation. I'm sure you want the culprits caught as much as I do."

She thought she heard sarcasm in his voice.

The detective had the officer by the door escort her out of the bedroom. In the living room, her cell phone rang, and as she stopped to answer it her escort was called away by a lab tech.

It was Drew on the line, wanting to know what was going on, if everyone was okay. She told him the news in a staid, *emotionless voice, worried she might throw up again if she let herself feel anything.*

"Oh God," Drew said. "Oh, baby, I'm so sorry. I'm coming over there. I'll pick you up."

She looked back toward the bedroom, saw someone unfolding a body bag, and turned away quickly. "No, don't," she told Drew. "I'm coming home. I don't want to be here."

"What happened?"

She fought back tears. It felt like her chest was going to explode. She wanted so badly to tell Drew the truth so she wouldn't have to carry the burden alone, but she couldn't bring herself to say the words. Maybe one day she could tell him the truth about the Dragon, and maybe he would even believe her, but not tonight. She couldn't handle anything more tonight. "It was random," she whispered into the phone. "A robbery. They surprised a robber."

It was the first time she'd lied outright to Drew, and now that she had, she knew it wouldn't be the last.

After the phone call, there was one more thing she had to do before she left. She knelt by the remains of one of the shelving units and sifted through the items on the floor. Under the broken wing of a porcelain angel she found a small picture frame, not much larger than a deck of cards. Inside was a photo of her mother and father standing outside the house. They were smiling. Proud. Happy. Alive. The glass front of the frame was broken and a spot of blood had landed on the picture, right at her father's forehead.

She opened the frame and removed the picture. She tried to wipe the blood away with her thumb, but it had already dried to a crust. She used her nail to chip away as much of it as she could, then slipped the photo into her wallet. There, she thought. Now they would always be with her.

She resumed her search, sifting through the debris, pile after pile, separating out the books from everything else, but she didn't find it. The Book of Ascalon was gone.

The meat puppets' shuffling footsteps came closer, the sound echoing off the warehouse walls. Only one shell left. Georgia tried to push away the fear that crawled in her belly like a spider. She pulled the shotgun close, her finger on the trigger, bringing the recoil pad toward her shoulder. She started counting to three, but all she pictured in her head was the horror in her parents' bedroom. Had it hurt? She tried counting to five. Did her parents suffer when the Dragon killed them? Would *Georgia* suffer? She decided to count to ten. She stared at the barrel of the shotgun and wondered if it would be better to kill herself with it. It probably wouldn't hurt—not as much as what the Dragon would do to her, anyway—and then everything would be over. She could have blanket peace forever.

When she reached ten, she spun and aimed the shotgun over the top of the table.

One of the meat puppets stood only a few feet away, pointing its gun in her direction. It was close enough for Georgia to see the trenches dug into its face where the Dragon had shredded the skin. The exposed jawbone made her think for a moment of Roy Dalton and his missing teeth. Then she looked at the gun in its hand.

She steadied the shotgun against her shoulder—*Don't*

miss, make it count!—and fired. The meat puppet's head blew apart and it fell limply to the floor.

Three, she thought. The shotgun was empty.

She crouched down again and surveyed the scene. Two of them moved through the shadows along the wall to her left. Three more were approaching from the right.

Georgia lay the shotgun on the floor as quietly as she could. She looked at the corpse lying just beyond the overturned table, at the automatic pistol it had dropped.

The others inched closer to her position.

Georgia sprang for the pistol. Her injured knee sent sparks of pain up her leg. It gave out in mid-stride, and she tumbled to the floor. Wincing, she reached for the gun. Her fingertips brushed the rubber grip, but it was too far to pick up. She heard a gunshot crack the air like a whip, felt something hot whiz past her scalp. A skull-faced meat puppet loomed over her, ready to fire again. She pulled herself forward along the floor, grabbed the gun and rolled onto her back, pulling the trigger three times. The bullets punched through its face and blew out the back of its head. It fell. She grabbed its pistol too and, with one in each hand, rose to her feet. She kept one pistol trained on the two meat puppets to her left and the other on the two to her right. She stood there, arms out like Christ on the cross, and wondered how many shots she could squeeze off before one of them put a bullet in her head, or her heart, or her belly. Her sore knee wobbled under her weight.

The meat puppets kept their guns trained on her, and the Dragon said, "You are persistent, child. I give you that. I have listened to so many beg for mercy that it surprises me when someone does not. What is it you want? What keeps you fighting?"

Georgia didn't plan on answering, but the words spilled out, surprising her. "You killed them."

"I have killed many."

"My father. My mother. Zack." She was breathing hard. Her hands shook. Her knee felt like it was going to crumple.

"It is the way," the Dragon said. "Your bloodline. You. Me. We are a knot. A tangle from which neither can break free. It has always been this way."

Her cheeks felt hot. She didn't realize she was crying until she felt the tears rolling down her face. "I don't care. You took *everything* from me!"

"So it is vengeance you seek? Am I not entitled to defend myself against those who hunt me? Who wish me dead?"

"Just show yourself!" she shouted. "You want to end this so badly? Come out and let's end it, face to face!"

"It is the right of every living creature to feed. To survive."

Georgia shook her head, and when she spoke her voice sounded cold even to her. "Not you."

"No?"

"You were supposed to die. George of Cappadocia—"

"He was a halfwit who could not see his own hand in front of his face," the Dragon said. "He thought his cross would protect him, but the silly trinket meant nothing to me. It is no surprise he failed. But ask yourself, child, *why* was I supposed to die? By what law was it decreed? Is it so terrible that I live? Is it so wrong to want to be whole?"

CHASING THE DRAGON

Georgia frowned. *Whole?* What did that mean?

"Tell me this, child. If I was supposed to die when that fool tried to spear my breast with his lance, why was I created at all? What would be the purpose of such an imprudent destiny?"

The same story told throughout time, she thought. No one knew why. Not even the Dragon, it seemed.

"Have you ever wondered, child, how long I have *actually* lived? Or do you really believe it all started with half-blind George and his terrible aim in the Fourth Century?"

The meat puppets on both sides moved closer, still training their guns on her. Her whole body trembled. She felt weak. She wasn't sure how much longer she could keep her arms extended with the guns growing heavier by the moment, or how long her knee would hold.

"Call them off! Now!"

"The game is finished," the Dragon said. "You lost. If destiny is so important to you, the time has come to accept yours."

Georgia pulled the trigger of the gun in her left hand. One of the meat puppets fell backward, but she'd only hit it in the chest. It would get back up, but at least she'd bought herself a few extra seconds. She turned and fired the gun in her right hand. The pistol gave a sad little click.

Shit.

She tossed the empty gun away and tried to run for the exit. All she could manage was a pathetic, hobbling limp.

This is how it ends, she thought. And then she thought, *I'm sorry, Dad. I tried. I really did.*

A gunshot cracked behind her. The bullet grazed her arm, stinging and hot. She struggled to stay on her feet and keep moving toward the open warehouse door, but her knee finally gave out, and she fell. Her chin hit the cement floor. Her teeth jangled in her mouth; her brain was a car slamming into the divider. She tried to get up, but it wasn't just her knee anymore. Now her whole leg had stopped obeying her, hanging off her body like dead weight. She put her palms on the floor and pushed herself up, but she was too weak and fell again.

In front of her was her overturned purse, its contents spilled on the floor, and beyond it was the exit. She'd been so close. She reached one shaking hand for the shaft of sunlight shining through the doorway. Then her hand fell to the cold cement with a slap.

Four pairs of sneakers entered her field of vision, walking toward her. Had someone come to rescue her? A moment of hope sparked in her chest, and she thought of Grace Kelly coming to Gary Cooper's aid at the end of *High Noon*. But then she blinked, focused, and saw the sneakers were spattered with blood. The meat puppets. No one was coming to help her. There was no cavalry on the way.

Her mind reeled, and she thought, *The walking dead in sneakers. That should be a commercial.* And then she thought of long dark tunnels with bright lights at the end, and wondered if her parents would be waiting for her.

One meat puppet grabbed her hair and pulled her up onto her knees. She winced and sucked air through her teeth. Then she lifted the loaded pistol still in her left hand and put it under its chin. If she was going to die, at least she'd take one last grey-skinned motherfucker with her. She pulled the trigger, and the bullet blew through its head. She laughed, or thought she did. The noise that came out of her mouth sounded desperate and crazy.

The twitching corpse let go of her hair. She pushed herself off the floor, forced herself to stand, favouring her injured leg.

She looked down at the gun in her hand and wondered if she had enough bullets to get out of there alive after all. More guns littered the floor near the meat puppets she'd shot. If she could reach them—

Movement caught her eye, and when she lifted her head she saw one coming at her, holding a small metal table by two of the legs. She was too slow bringing up the gun. The meat puppet swung the table, and it slammed against her, knocking her backward into the wall. The back of her head struck the cinderblocks. She slid down and landed on her knees. Fireworks exploded behind her eyes, and she collapsed.

The floor was cold against her cheek. Other than that she couldn't feel much. She struggled to keep her eyes open, but sticky blood covered half her face, sealing one shut. The blood was definitely hers this time. She felt it oozing out of a cut in her scalp.

She saw the meat puppets' sneakers again. She decided she hated sneakers. She would never buy another pair. Something about that made her want to laugh her crazy laugh again, but she was too weak to do anything except watch the sneakers and wait for the sound of the final gunshot.

But they didn't come toward her. They backed away instead. Foolish of her to think the meat puppets would finish her off. The Dragon would want to do that with her own hands.

Then she heard it, the sound of something heavy moving across the floor. A pungent odour hung in the air, growing stronger as the steps came closer. The scent of an ancient creature, it smelled of dust and earth and corruption. A long hem of frayed brown cloth glided into view before her, dragging along the floor. The odour was overpowering. Uncontrollable fear shook Georgia's body. She felt something sharp touch her cheek. A talon.

She squeezed her eye shut and felt tears run down her nose. *Oh God, Daddy, I'm sorry!*

With a lover's intimacy, the talon traced lazy circles on Georgia's cheek. "Do you know what I love most about this modern age, child?" Coming from the Dragon's own mouth instead of through the meat puppets, her voice sounded strange, like an orchestra suddenly reduced to a single violin. "Humanity has finally learned what I have known for centuries. You have learned patience. You have learned to *wait*. Once upon a time, you were in such a rush. It made sense, I suppose. Your lifespan was shorter than it is now. Now you can wait for just . . ." the talon tapped against her cheek, and Georgia flinched, "the right," another tap, "moment," a third tap, and Georgia let out a terrified moan.

"Now you wait until you have everything in order—a job, a home, a stable marriage—before you decide to continue your bloodline. Did you know when your great-great-grandfather was your age, he had already sired five sons?" The Dragon sighed, and Georgia felt hot breath blow against her. "Succulent as lambs, all of them. They tasted of pepper and steel. And your father, when he was your age his wife already carried you in her womb. But that is not the case with you, child. You are the last of the bloodline. There will be no more after you. No one left to stop me. It ends here, now, in this room. And no one will ever know."

She felt the talon leave her cheek and saw the Dragon's long, yellowing claws, crusted with dirt, pick through the spilled contents of her purse.

"I feel you when you dream," the Dragon said. "Perhaps you did not know. Every night, when the part of me that is inside you spreads through your veins, I taste the despair in your thoughts. And when that despair turns to desperation, I taste something else. Something that is at first chemical and sharp, then sweet. As warm and smooth as honey, yet something I have never tasted before."

The Dragon's claws closed around the rolled-up leather pack and lifted it from the floor.

Georgia heard the Dragon fumbling to open it and moaned, "No. Give it back!" She started shaking again. An insistent itch spread over her skin. *One more fix, just one more before I die.*

"Our minds are linked," the Dragon said. "The knot I spoke of. The tangle from which we cannot break free. I know you look through my eyes when I kill. I feel you inside me, and I take a great deal of pleasure in the thought that you are forced to watch the agony of my prey. And so it is only fair that I am inside you in return. It is hazy and confused, yes, but this bag, I see it often. It intrigues me how its contents make you dream. How it holds you in its grip so firmly. It must have a very powerful taste."

"Give it back," she tried to say, but what came out of her mouth was a desperate animal bleating. She wanted to snatch the pack out of the Dragon's grasp, but her arm only flopped at her side.

"You see? Even in your last moments, you can think of nothing else. You cannot even pray. It must be a powerful taste indeed."

Georgia heard the leather pack roll open and saw the hypodermic fall on the floor in front of her. It bounced, and the blue plastic cap came off the needle. The hypodermic rolled to a stop by her hand.

"What is this?" the Dragon demanded. "Nothing but useless trinkets. There is no meat. No marrow. Show me, child, and you will live another few minutes. Show me how to devour this."

Georgia snatched the hypodermic off the floor. With the last bit of strength in her body, she jammed the needle through the brown cloth and into what she hoped was the Dragon's foot. She definitely hit *something*. She'd meant it only as a final act of defiance, but to her surprise the Dragon howled a high-pitched wail of pain that she thought would split her skull. The meat puppets threw back their heads and echoed the Dragon's cry. The floor shook. Cracks tore in the walls.

And then the Dragon was gone, a blurred shadow disappearing through the warehouse door and into the brilliant sizzle of sunlight.

The bright doorway dimmed along with everything else.

I got her, Georgia thought, even as she wondered how something as small as the needle could cause the Dragon such pain. *I made her hurt; that's all that matters. She'll remember that. She'll always remember how bad I hurt her before I died.*

Then she fell into the dark.

6.

THE EARTH CRUMBLES WHERE SHE TREADS

Georgia thought she might be dreaming. She thought she might be dead. She was sure someone was standing in the middle of the warehouse floor, watching her. She could tell it was a man from his silhouette, but he was as dark as a shadow. She couldn't see his face. He held something flat and square in his hands.

"Get up," he said. The familiar voice raised goosebumps on her arms.

Dad?

"Get up, Georgia," he said. He stepped forward, and the shadows fell back from her father's face.

Is it really you?

"I need you to get up."

Daddy?

She trembled. She thought she might be crying.

What he was holding was a folded blue blanket, as bright and fresh as the day he'd bought it for her.

"I can't," she said. Her voice was a sandpaper whisper. It hurt to speak.

I'm sorry, Dad. I didn't mean to be like this. I just wanted to make you proud, but I did everything wrong. I couldn't kill the Dragon. I couldn't stop her from killing you and mom. And now I'm alone and I think I'm dying and there won't be anyone left.

He bent over her and spread the blanket. It settled warmly around her, and suddenly the warehouse was gone and she was girl again, five years old and back in her childhood bedroom . . .

The morning sun streamed through the crack in the curtains. The blue Snoopy blanket was still bunched around her neck from the night before, when she'd been afraid vampires would get her in her sleep. Her father stood over her, trying to persuade her to get out of bed, but she wouldn't. She was angry at him for disappearing for two whole days and making her mother worried and scared. Just last night, unable to sleep, she'd crept to the living room doorway and seen her mother sitting on the couch, comforting herself with one of her porcelain angels the way Georgia had secretly seen her do many times before. Her mother stroked its wings and whispered, "Bring him back to us. Please bring him back safely," and then she'd noticed Georgia and snapped angrily at her to go back to bed. Now, in the morning, her father was finally back, and Georgia was punishing him the only way she knew how—by refusing to get out of bed.

"I promise I'll make it up to you," her father said. "If you want, we can spend all day playing tag in the woods out back, you and me and your mom. Besides, it's the last day of the weekend. Tomorrow you have to go back to school. So you'd better get up already."

She pouted and crossed her arms under the blanket. "I don't like when you're not here."

"I'm here now," he said.

"What about tomorrow? And the day after that? Are you gonna go away again and not even call?"

His jaw tightened and he got a funny, faraway look in his eye. "I'm sorry," he said. "I didn't mean to make you worry about me. Someday, when you're old enough, I'll explain to you what happened, why I go away sometimes. I promise. But right now, I need you to get up."

"No, I'm tired." She pretended to yawn. In truth, she was wide awake and hungry for breakfast, but she didn't want him to know that.

"Get up, Georgia." He tickled her, and she laughed and kicked her legs under the blanket.

"Why should I?" she asked, trying to remain defiant.

"Because I said so. I'm your father and you have to do what I say. It's the rules."

She thought about that for a moment and said, "If I have to do what you say and get up, then you have to do what I say. Deal?"

He stroked his chin the way he always did when he was pretending to think really hard about something important.

"Deal. But just for a few minutes. Then I want you out of bed and at the breakfast table, missy."

That was the day her favourite game, Do What Georgia Says, was invented. She looked up at her father and stroked her chin just like him.

"Clap your hands," she said, and he did.

"Bark like a dog," she said, and he did.

"Live forever," she said.

"I need you to get up, Georgia," her father said again as the warehouse came rushing back to her.

"I can't," she sobbed. Her body felt like a stone. Dead weight.

"Get up."

She pushed her palms against the floor. Her elbows wobbled, gave out, and she fell. "I can't!" The words came out in a scream.

Her father said, "You have to do what I say. It's the rules."

She pushed against the floor again.

"Get up, Georgia."

Her elbows held this time, and she was able to slide her knees beneath her. The hurt one flared up for a moment, and she winced in pain. She forced herself to stand, one foot on the floor, then the other. She steadied herself. Her injured leg felt numb, her knee swollen. Her head hurt where she'd struck the wall.

"Now *you* have to do what *I* say," she told him, but when she looked up her father and the blanket were gone. She took in the room around her and remembered where she was. Five meat puppets lay on the floor where she'd shot them. The three others were gone. They must have followed the Dragon out the door.

That was the second time the Dragon had nearly killed her, only to flee in pain before the final blow. Georgia still didn't understand why.

She limped toward the open doorway, hoping her car was still outside. The morning brightness had dimmed to a murky twilight. She must have been unconscious for hours.

The Dragon could be anywhere by now, miles from Buckshot Hill, and Georgia would have to start the chase all over again. It was just as well. She was so tired she doubted she could do anything but flop onto the bed at the motel and sleep for days.

She accidentally kicked her purse, having forgotten it was there, and it slid a couple of inches along the floor. She bent down to retrieve it and noticed that the leather pack was gone. Then she remembered—the Dragon had still been holding the pack when she fled the warehouse. The heroin was gone. The needle she'd stuck in the Dragon's foot was gone. Her addiction roared inside her, furious at being denied, and the image in her mind of dead grey skin spreading out from her hip caused fear to mushroom in her belly. She wanted to lose control, to kick the floor and punch the walls, but she didn't have the energy. All she could do was stand there with a sinking heart. Without the heroin, she was as good as dead. The Dragon had killed her after all.

She pulled herself together, remembered where she was. The Inkheads' stash house. The Inkheads sold drugs.

CHASING THE DRAGON

The floor suddenly swayed and shuddered beneath her. The cracks in the walls grew longer, sending chips of cement rattling to the floor. Entropy, the Dragon's calling card. The warehouse could come down at any moment. She was lucky it hadn't already, or the collapse would have buried her alive. If she was going to find more heroin, she'd have to be fast.

She limped through the open door through which the meat puppets had spilled earlier. In the back of the building, the walls that had originally separated the management offices had been knocked down, leaving a single, mammoth room almost as large as the warehouse out front. She found four more bodies slumped just past the door, not enough of them left for the Dragon to resurrect as meat puppets. Georgia stepped over the remains, trying not to look too closely.

Big, domed lamps hung from the ceiling on long chains. Iron-barred windows were set high in the walls. Below them backpacks, puffy eight-ball jackets, spent shells and discarded handguns lay scattered on the floor amid pools of blood. A series of tables had been set up around the perimeter of the room with digital scales, mounds of plastic baggies and stainless steel apothecary chests. She limped toward them, the cramps of dope sickness already starting to tie her insides into knots, and suddenly the floor reared up toward her. The tables, the windows, the whole room tilted away. Georgia's feet were off the ground. At first she thought she was flying and figured she was dead after all, sailing off to that dark tunnel with the bright light, but then she realized she was in fact sliding backward down a slope of loose dirt. Her back hit something hard and seized painfully for a moment. She squeezed her eyes shut until the pain subsided, then opened them and saw dirt all around her, and the ceiling high above.

A hole. She'd fallen into a hole. Not a sinkhole like the kind that formed wherever the Dragon went, but something different. She climbed back up the slope to the top and saw that she had fallen into a deep trench that ran the length of the room. An excavation, as though something large had been dug out of the floor. The edges were ragged, not squared off the way they would be if shovels or heavy digging equipment had been used. The Dragon had done this, she realized. She'd seen the dirt on her claws. The Dragon had torn through the floor, ripped open the earth and removed . . . what? What had been down there?

A long crack ripped violently through in the ceiling, startling her, and plaster dust fell in gritty white curtains. The fracture spread quickly, spiderwebbing above her, and the lamps shivered on their chains. The building shook again. The whole warehouse was about to come down.

She turned away, back toward the door she'd come through. There was no time to search the stash. She limped as quickly as she could out of the back room, ignoring another cramp tightening in her stomach. She grabbed her shotgun off the floor—there was no time to collect the spent shells now—snatched up her purse and forced her aching legs to carry her out of the building. She managed to just reach her car when the warehouse fell in on itself. A huge cloud of dust blew outward from the collapse. She ducked down behind the car, her knee searing with pain again, and shielded herself until the cloud dissipated. When she stood up, there was nothing left of the Bristleman Corp. warehouse but a pile of rubble.

She expected to hear the sound of panicked voices, the rush of feet, but there was nothing. Not even sirens. The streets stayed quiet. Deserted.

She thought of going back to Egg Foo for more heroin, but she was out of cash. She had to think of something. If she didn't get her hands on more soon, it would be over. The Dragon would win.

The pavement between her car and the collapsed warehouse shuddered and split open. The sinkhole was spreading. She got into her car, twisted the key in the ignition and took off. In the rearview mirror, she saw the spot where she'd parked buckle and plunge into the earth.

Navigating the streets of the warehouse district in the dimming light, she wondered how long she had left to live. The infection only seemed to spread at night, and night was coming fast. Without heroin to beat it back, she wouldn't see the dawn. She could go after the Dragon, try to get it back, but she was too weak to fight her. The fastest way to get her hands on the drug now would be to steal it. The Shaolin Tong would be too heavily armed to risk trying to rob them. Where else? There were no other drug dealers in Buckshot Hill now that the Inkheads were dead, their stash buried under who knew how many tons of rubble.

Think, dammit!

A hospital. She could pull into an emergency room in her blood-soaked clothes and say, *I hurt my head, I hurt my knee*, and then when the doctors turned their backs she could sneak away, find the drug repository and nab some morphine. Would morphine work? But she didn't know where the Buckshot Hill hospital was, or even if it had one, and she was so tired. The doctors would know right away. One look at her and they'd know she was a junkie and put armed guards around her so she didn't steal any drugs, and while she was lying there waiting for them to return, the infection would keep spreading until she was dead. They would come back to find her corpse in the examination room, grey and black-veined and moving under the Dragon's control, and god she was so tired she just wanted to sleep.

She forced her mind to keep sifting through her options, but she kept coming up empty. She didn't have any heroin, and there was nothing she could do about it. It was high noon and she'd arrived at the showdown only to find her gun empty.

On the road back into town, the blacktop was as cracked as parched earth. Chunks of pavement dropped away all around her. She swerved to avoid the sinkholes as they appeared and willed her eyes to stay open just a little longer. She could rest soon, she told herself. Soon all the pain and grief and terror would be over.

A dark grey fog rolled in from nowhere and enveloped the car, suddenly limiting her visibility to only a few feet. She slowed, her stiff knee protesting as she worked the brake. A sharp odour seeped in around the closed windows, and she realized it wasn't fog. It was smoke. In the distance, she saw muffled lights crackling like lightning. A fire somewhere.

A big, dark silhouette moved through the smoke toward her car. She watched the shape approach, gripping the steering wheel until her knuckles turned white. Then the smoke parted and a chestnut brown horse cantered through, the white stripe along its nose reflecting her headlights. It clip-clopped past the car like a phantom, not even looking in her direction, and disappeared into the smoke beyond.

Georgia drove on, maintaining a slow speed through the almost impenetrable smoke. As the lights grew closer, she realized she was looking at a house on fire. The land all around it was cracked and sunken. Beside the house was a flaming structure that looked like it had once been a stable, and next to it she saw a sinkhole and what looked like the exploded remains of several propane canisters. At least the horse had gotten out. She hoped the family had too.

A crowd had gathered on the opposite side of the road to watch the firefighters tackle the blaze. A black and white highway patrol car was parked in front of them, its siren lights spinning red and blue in the haze and making the number 113 painted on its side glow like a digital clock. Two State Troopers stood next to the car in their navy and grey uniforms. One was speaking into the radio handset. The other turned to watch Georgia's car, kept watching as she passed. He had a moustache and tired eyes. She glanced in the rearview mirror and saw him vanish in the smoke.

Georgia caught a glimpse of herself in the rearview. She was covered in blood—her face, her hair, her clothes. One of her cheeks sported a dark bruise. Had the Trooper seen her? Was that why he'd stared at her when she drove by? She felt a moment of panic, thought of the shotgun shells in the warehouse rubble near the bodies, how easily the authorities could trace everything back to her, and then let it go. The State Troopers had their hands full tonight, and by morning it wouldn't matter if they came looking for her.

Downtown Buckshot Hill was deserted. The smoke had begun to dissipate, turning into a grey mist that rolled over the sidewalks and across the storefronts. A long crack climbed up the side of a women's boutique, etching thin fissures into the glass of the front window. A varsity jacket lay discarded on the sidewalk. Two of the tables in front of the ice cream parlour were overturned onto their sides. She'd never seen the devastation spread this far before.

Georgia thought of the enormous hole dug into the floor of the warehouse. She'd always assumed the Dragon's movements were random, that she went wherever she could hide safely and feed in secret. Her ancestors had chased the Dragon through Africa, Asia and Europe, and finally to America. She'd believed all along that the Dragon was simply running from them, but what if the Dragon's travels weren't arbitrary? What if she was looking for something?

There was no more smoke by the time Georgia pulled into the Buckshot Motor Inn's parking lot, but the smell of burning wood was still in the air. No one stood on the porch outside the rooms. Marcus Townsend's car was back in its spot, a child-sized trucker hat printed with the words RIO ARRIBA FAIRBOARD RANCH RODEO sitting in the back seat, but the windows of his room were dark. The slam of her car door sounded thunderously loud in the quiet of the parking lot. Nothing moved. No lights came on.

She took her purse and the shotgun and let herself into her room. There, she dropped everything at the foot of the bed, peeled off her bloodstained clothes and stood under the hottest shower she could stand. Her muscles ached. Her sore knee looked twice as big as the other and had turned shades of yellow and purple. A red line crossed her deltoid muscle where the bullet had grazed her, and the cut on her forehead was tender to the touch. Standing in front of the bathroom mirror, towelling herself off and wincing with each sore movement, the dope sickness hit her again, twisting her gut. She knelt over the toilet and dry-heaved until her ribs hurt. She'd never felt more defeated. More alone.

Finally, she collapsed on the bed in her sweat shorts and t-shirt. She rolled down the waistband and saw her scarred hip had started to turn grey again. Soon the infection would travel outward, down her leg, across her torso, until it filled her completely. She found herself trembling, but she didn't know if it was from fear or from jonesing.

Georgia took a deep breath, wondering how many more she had left. She turned off the light, lay back and closed her eyes. What point was there in fighting it? She couldn't think of a reason *not* to let the infection take her. She was a failure. She'd failed in her relationships. She'd failed her parents. She'd failed to kill the Dragon. She'd failed to have children and ensure the lineage of dragonslayers continued after her. She might as well do everyone a favour and die.

She will devour the world. That's what the Book of Ascalon had said about the Dragon. Well, it was all hers now.

She could choke on it.

A loud bang woke her. She hadn't realized she'd fallen asleep. She was drenched in sweat. It was still dark outside. She shifted on the bed, rolled over. She just wanted to sleep. The bang came again. Loud. The motel room door. She switched on the light and, with her stiff knee complaining, swung her heavy legs over the side of the bed. The grey patch on her skin had grown, the veins turning black beneath it. She poked at it sleepily. It was numb. Dead skin. Dead Georgia.

Another bang, and the door broke off its hinges and crashed to the floor. Startled, she fell off the bed. Staying crouched, she peeked over the mattress to see what was happening.

A tall figure walked into the room, shrouded in a dark brown cloak. The opening in the large, drooping hood was deeply shadowed, obscuring the face within. The hands that reached up to pull back the hood were scaly and ended not with fingers but with long, curved claws like ancient, yellowing ivory. "Found you, child," the Dragon said.

The window beside the door shattered, and dozens of dead, grey arms reached through.

7.

SHE WILL DEVOUR THE WORLD

*Curled up on the couch next to her father, Georgia looked at
the painting in the Book of Ascalon. There was Saint George
in his black armour, his horse rearing as his lance plunged
into the Dragon's chest, and in the background, the woman
who sat on the tall rocks.*

"So, Daddy, who's that woman if she's not a princess?"

*"The artist, Gustave Moreau, was commissioned to paint
this by our family, back in the 1800s when they lived in Paris,"
he said. "They told him exactly what to paint, down to the
last detail. But none of what you see here is actually what
happened in Cyrene."*

*Thinking she finally understood, she looked up at him.
"There was no princess, was there?"*

He ruffled her hair. "Smart kid. No, there was no princess."

"*Then who is she? Why did they want her in the picture?*"

"*It's a secret code. A warning. Remember those illustrations we saw, how the Dragon didn't look the same in all of them? She's different each time she comes back. She . . . evolves.*" He handed her the book. "*Look closely at Saint George's eyes. What is he looking at?*"

She brought the book close to her face and discovered that though Saint George's head was tipped toward the creature on the ground, his eyes were looking elsewhere. She followed his gaze in a straight line, all the way to the woman.

"*That's her, Georgia,*" *her father said.* "*That's the Dragon.*"

The thing standing in the doorway of Georgia's motel room was a mockery of a human being. The Dragon's face still had the flat nose and wide, lipless mouth of a reptile, despite her strangely human eyes and the few limp strands of auburn hair that sprouted from her otherwise bald cranium. She didn't have ears, just holes on the sides of her skull. The cloak bulged out in front of her where her huge stomach sagged to her knees, full of the meat and gristle of those she'd slaughtered.

The Dragon had grown decrepit in her advanced age. Her scaled skin was tinged a sickly green, no longer the leathery armour it must have been back in the Fourth Century. Now it looked as thin and brittle as tissue paper. Her talons had grown so long and heavy over the centuries that they weighed her hands down from her wrists.

CHASING THE DRAGON

Georgia had seen a lot of terrible things, but nothing so awful as the toothsome, triumphant grin on the Dragon's face.

Meat puppets crawled in through the broken window and lumbered through the doorway. Georgia grabbed the stock of the shotgun at the foot of the bed and slid it toward her. The box of shells sat on the floor next to her suitcase, across the room. She glanced quickly at the meat puppets spilling past where the Dragon stood. They were slow, but that wouldn't buy her much time in the small room. She broke open the shotgun, sprang for the ammo box and fumbled with the shells. They spilled out at her feet. She reached for one and gasped to see black veins marbling her legs, the skin already paling to grey. She scooped up the shells and started loading them into the shotgun, trying not to shake.

"Can you feel me growing inside you, child?" the Dragon asked. "I can. I can taste the fear in your thoughts."

The meat puppets kept coming. She couldn't tell how many there were. Ten? Fifteen? The shotgun only held six shells at a time. It wouldn't be enough. But if this was her last stand, she'd go down swinging.

Georgia snapped the shotgun closed and rolled back behind the bed, clumsy from her stiff knee. She pumped the first shell into the chamber and took aim at the closest meat puppet. It had been an Inkhead, the black bandana tied tight above the loose, shredded skin of its face.

If you can really taste my thoughts, taste this one! She pulled the trigger, blasting the meat puppet's head into a chunky smear on the wallpaper behind it. The others moved forward to take its place as it slumped to the floor, and she pivoted quickly to sight down the barrel at the next one.

Oh no, not him . . .

It was a black man, or had been once, before its skin had turned a pallid grey. Blood from the open wound on its throat smeared across the writing on its t-shirt: RIO ARRIBA FAIRBOARD RANCH RODEO. Marcus Townsend, her car-loving neighbour from the room next door.

He'd been nice to her. He'd talked with her outside and given her a brief but welcome taste of normality in her nightmarish excuse for a life. It shamed her, thinking how she'd jonesed in front of him and ran out in the middle of their conversation, and now she'd never have a chance to apologize to him, to make things right.

It lurched toward her, its dead fingers groping.

Georgia took a deep breath to steel herself and pulled the trigger. The face that had once belonged to Marcus Townsend exploded, and the headless corpse toppled backward to the floor.

Behind where it had stood was another, a small boy of nine or ten. It wore a t-shirt with a cowboy riding a bucking bronco. Both its arms were gone. Bloody stumps filled the t-shirt's sleeves. Its face was as blank and terrible as its father's had been.

Instinctively, she took her finger off from the trigger. A child. Just a child . . .

"I brought my boy with me this time 'round. He's old enough now that I thought I'd make a vacation out of it, show him some of the country so he doesn't think it's all high

rises and housing projects, you know?"

She shook Marcus's voice out of her head and let her training take over. *Don't hesitate. If you hesitate, it'll kill you.* Georgia swallowed hard and replaced her finger on the trigger. *It's not really him. He's dead. He's an empty shell, not a boy. Not Marcus's son.* She swallowed again. Her trigger finger twitched. She couldn't do it. Not a child. The tiny meat puppet stumbled closer, off balance without its arms. Her heart felt like it was going to shatter into pieces. *Just close your fucking eyes and shoot!*

She did, and after the loud bang of the shotgun she heard him fall. When she opened her eyes, she saw the boy had fallen at his father's feet. She felt like crying.

Another had circled around the bed. A fat blonde woman in a tight tube top. Georgia recognized her right away, despite her mutilated face. The garish red lipstick she'd worn while showing Georgia her room in the Shaolin Tong warehouse was replaced by a glistening smear of blood. Her bottom jaw hung loose, her tongue lolling out.

First Marcus and now her. The Dragon must have retraced Georgia's steps while she'd lain unconscious in the Inkheads' warehouse, the visions of their deaths swallowed up by the blackness. The Dragon had killed them for no other reason than that Georgia knew them, had purposely surrounded herself with an army of familiar corpses to keep Georgia off her guard. It was monstrous.

Georgia raised the shotgun toward the blonde meat puppet. It knocked the barrel aside and grabbed for her. Georgia leapt up onto the bed, intending to jump down on the other side, but her stiff knee slowed her. The meat puppet grabbed her by the hair and pulled Georgia toward it. She hit it in the chest with the butt of the shotgun and slipped free, falling backward onto the bed. She jammed the barrel into the ragged gash of its mouth.

Georgia pulled the trigger. Cold, thick blood spattered across her face. The shock and disgust kept her momentarily frozen in place. She thought of fish swimming like silhouettes in a deep blue light.

Move! Move, dammit!

Wiping the blood out of her eyes, she rolled off the bed.

And smacked right into another one. It wore a yellow bandana on its head and had the Shaolin Tong symbol tattooed on its arm. It was missing a great deal of skin from the right side of its face, leaving one round white eye like a ping-pong ball staring out at her from the blood and tissue. There was so much blood on its clothing she almost didn't notice the gashes where his chest had been ripped open. It pinned her arms to her side with strong, vise-like hands and lifted her off the ground. Unable to raise the shotgun to line up a shot, she kicked it in the groin, in the stomach, but it didn't do any good. The dead felt no pain. She swung her legs back until she felt her toes touch the bed. She placed her feet flat on the mattress, bent her one good knee and pushed off, sending the meat puppet tumbling backward with its arms still around her. It landed on its back, and the force of the impact knocked its eye loose and sent it rolling down its cheek to the carpet. Georgia landed on top of the meat puppet and squirmed out of its grasp. It started to get back up, groping blindly for her, but she put the barrel to its forehead and blew its head apart.

There was only one shell left in the shotgun. There was no way she'd have time to reload before they overpowered her. She had to make the last shot count. She looked at the seemingly endless army of meat puppets shambling toward her, and behind them, the Dragon, watching Georgia with her too-human eyes. She looked almost amused.

How many had the Dragon killed? Not over the centuries, she thought, just tonight. Just for this final ambush. Just to have an army between her and Georgia.

Her jaw tightened, and she took a step toward the Dragon. She'd fight her way through a hundred meat puppets if she had to. A thousand. It didn't matter if she only had one shell left. She was going to take that cold-blooded bitch down.

A small hand grabbed the shotgun's barrel. Egg Foo. The oversized Lobos jersey had been shredded open, revealing frayed skin underneath. The gold chain around its neck was caked with dried blood. The sunglasses sat lopsided on its face.

Another hand, a fist this time, came out of nowhere, connecting with her jaw. She reeled back, stunned, and Egg Foo yanked the shotgun out of her hand, tossed it aside. Then it grabbed one of her arms, and whoever had punched her grabbed the other. Together they pulled her upright, and she saw the second meat puppet was Roy Dalton. The motel owner's torso had been torn open, and as it yanked her forward, Georgia felt the wet red things hanging out of its belly touch her. She fought back a gag.

The two meat puppets pulled her toward the doorway, where the Dragon waited. Georgia dug her feet into the carpet and tried to resist, but the meat puppets were stronger. The dead didn't weaken, didn't tire. The others moved aside, forming a corridor with the Dragon at its end.

"At last," the Dragon said. A long red tongue, forked like a snake's, dipped out of her mouth.

Egg Foo and Roy Dalton shoved Georgia to the floor, holding her arms behind her painfully. It felt like her shoulders were going to snap out of their sockets. Above her, Georgia saw the Dragon raise her heavy talons.

A loud, electronic squawk startled Georgia, and she glanced past the Dragon out the door. A black and white highway patrol car had pulled into the motel parking lot, the number 113 painted on its side. The same car she'd seen at the burning house, when the moustached State Trooper had watched her drive by covered in blood. With a rush of relief, she realized he'd come looking for her after all.

The Trooper and his partner exited the patrol car. She saw them point and say something to each other, but she couldn't hear what. Their hands dropped tentatively to their sidearms, but they stood where they were. Her heart sank. They didn't know what was happening. They were trying to take it all in, figure out the situation, but she didn't have time, she needed them *now*.

"Help!" she shouted. "Help me!"

The Dragon hissed and drew back a claw to strike her, but it was too late. The Troopers pulled their guns, and the one with the moustache shouted, "Hey!"

CHASING THE DRAGON

The meat puppets turned and marched out the doorway toward them. Only Egg Foo and Roy Dalton remained, holding Georgia in place. She tried to wriggle loose, but their grip was too strong. The Dragon leaned forward with that awful, toothsome smile again. Her tongue flicked out and hit Georgia's neck like wet sandpaper. Georgia squirmed.

"Just a taste before the meal," the Dragon said.

Through the doorway, Georgia saw the meat puppets advance on the patrol car. The Troopers ordered them not to come any closer and fired warning shots into the air. The walking corpses didn't stop. When the Troopers finally saw what they were, the colour drained from their faces. They fired into the crowd. Two meat puppets fell from lucky shots to the head, but the Troopers were still outnumbered. They reached the first Trooper and swarmed over him in a wave of grey flesh. Georgia heard him screaming. The moustached Trooper fired off a few panicked shots, hitting nothing, and ran around to the other side of the car.

His partner's screams stopped abruptly. The meat puppets left his broken, bleeding body on the pavement and began moving to the other side of the car. The moustached Trooper fired off a few more rounds, then grabbed the radio handset on the dashboard to call for backup. They surrounded him before he could pull it to his mouth, and brought him down.

Georgia felt a single talon against her neck.

"You were a good warrior, child," the Dragon breathed into her ear. "You fought almost as well as your predecessors."

The Trooper crawled out from under the meat puppets, his face bruised and bloody. He scrambled for the radio again, but then the meat puppets were on him, pulling him back. He struggled to the side of the car and grabbed something. The hinged lid over the gas tank, she realized. He opened it and fought against the meat puppets to unscrew the cap. They pulled at him with blood-covered hands and crowded over him again. The Trooper grit his teeth, lifted his handgun and inserted the muzzle into the open gas tank.

The Dragon's talon pressed against the skin of Georgia's neck and began to scrape across her throat. Georgia closed her eyes. She heard a muffled gunshot. The explosion was so loud it left her ears ringing, the light bright enough to penetrate her eyelids. She opened her eyes just as a shockwave of hot air knocked her down.

She lost sight of the Dragon. Her arms were free. A billowing cloud of smoke and flame rose from the wreckage of the patrol car. The meat puppets were on fire. Burning fragments of metal fell from the sky and pummelled the parking lot, the porch, the roof.

Georgia struggled to her feet and ran limping back into the room, over the corpses and sticky pools of blood and brain matter that covered the carpet. The shotgun lay where Egg Foo had dropped it by the bed. She lifted it and spun around. The Dragon was right behind, Roy Dalton at her side. She didn't see Egg Foo anywhere.

Georgia pumped the final shell into the chamber, aimed for the Dragon's head and fired. Roy stepped in front, intercepting the shot. The meat puppet's head burst into a pulpy mess, and its body was blown backward into the Dragon. Spattered with blood, the Dragon pushed the limp corpse to the floor and advanced on Georgia.

She flipped the shotgun over, gripping the barrel tight, and ran at the Dragon. She swung the shotgun like a baseball bat. Its heavy wooden stock connected with the Dragon's face. A long, sharp tooth fell out of her mouth on a strand of blood. The Dragon spat onto the floor and regarded Georgia with narrowed eyes, wiped her scaly chin with the back of her claw.

"My turn," she hissed.

Georgia didn't wait for her to make a move. She swung the shotgun again. This time the Dragon caught it and yanked it from her hands. She held the shotgun in one claw and with the other cleaved it easily in two where the barrel met the stock. Then she tossed the pieces aside.

Before Georgia could run, the Dragon lashed out, backhanding her across the cheek. She flew across the room until she felt the wall slam against her back, hitting so hard she bit her cheek and tasted blood. She stumbled against the bedside table, tripped over a dead meat puppet and fell. She looked up from the floor and saw the Dragon coming toward her.

The doorway. It wasn't far, but with each step the Dragon took, her chance of escape dwindled. She pushed herself to her feet and ran for the door, her knee aching and threatening to lock up on her. The Dragon swiped at her, her talons slicing nothing but air.

Georgia kept moving, pushing herself through the doorway. In the parking lot outside, she saw the flaming shell of the patrol car surrounded by charred corpses. The stench of burning meat and metal was overpowering. She turned on the porch, ready to keep running. grey arms wrapped tightly around her from behind. Over her shoulder she saw the oversized sunglasses on Egg Foo's slack, dead face.

The Dragon walked calmly out of the motel room. "You still do not understand, child. There is no place to run. No place that will be safe. This world is mine. It always has been, and always will be, mine."

Georgia fought the meat puppet's hold on her, but it was too strong. "It's not," she said feebly. "It's not yours."

The Dragon laughed. "Oh, but it is. Do you truly believe I came into this world with no greater destiny than to be killed by George the dragonslayer? Do you think that is all I am? I have had seventeen hundred years since then to consider the full measure of my destiny."

The ground shook suddenly. Cracks split the asphalt of the parking lot as if another sinkhole were forming.

"They came to me first as dreams," the Dragon continued. "Whispers of the great dragons from ages past. Only later did I realize these were not dreams, but memories. They told me of how I had trod upon this world in many forms throughout the ages, each time reborn with no memory of the past, each time murdered by the dragonslayer before the memories could resurface. But not this time. This time I lived. This time I *remembered*. Who I was. Who I am. What I had to do.

"Even your father helped in his own small way. When I came to his home, he fought so hard to protect a book in his possession that I knew it must be of great importance. I took it with me when I was finished with him and your wailing mother. Such a wonderful book! Its pages revealed to me my many forgotten names. Fafnir. Jörmungandr. Vritra. Illuyankas."

The cracks spread across the parking lot, and Georgia quickly realized it was no sinkhole. Instead of buckling, the ground swelled upward in a titanic dome of earth, stone and concrete. Something was being pushed up through the ground. Something so big that as it grew it knocked the burning patrol car onto its side and sent it scraping across the lot.

"And Tiamat," the Dragon said. "Mighty Tiamat, from whose bones Marduk created the world."

The mound exploded. Georgia flinched as chunks of concrete rained everywhere, pounding the porch roof and pummelling her car. Long white shapes flew from the hole in the ground, tumbling upward into the air.

"Ever since the memories returned, I have walked this world with a purpose," the Dragon said. "To be whole again. To reclaim what is rightfully mine. They sang to me from where they were buried, called me to them, desperate to be found. I dug each of them from the earth myself, freed them from their bonds. Now they heed *my* call. They follow me, eager to be rejoined. To be whole."

Georgia watched the white shapes fly up out of the hole and lock together like puzzle pieces. A horrible coldness settled over her when she realized what they were.

"The bones of Tiamat," the Dragon said. "The bones of the world. *My* bones."

The deep trench in the back room of the Inkheads' warehouse. The Dragon hadn't been hiding when she sent the meat puppets after her. They'd been a distraction to keep Georgia busy and give the Dragon time to finish digging.

She thought back to the roadside diner outside Buckshot Hill. The meat puppet there, the fry cook, had come from the kitchen. If she'd had time to check the kitchen before the building came down, would she have found a similar trench there? The roadhouse in North Carolina, a bordello in Memphis, an after-hours nightclub in Little Rock, all the other buildings she'd seen destroyed by sinkholes after the Dragon killed everyone inside—had there been bones beneath them all?

Her ancestors had been wrong. They'd thought entropy was something that emanated from the Dragon herself, but it wasn't. It was a result of her actions. She'd dug up the bones of the world.

The levitating bones continued fitting together, forming a skeleton that grew bigger and bigger. It took Georgia a moment to make sense of the shape they were creating: a long, serpentine spinal column that stretched across the parking lot and into the road beyond; great fingers of bone rising from its back like wings; six stocky legs that ended in fearsome claws; a neck that extended hundreds of feet into the sky.

A dragon. A true dragon.

"It took centuries to complete my task, gathering the bones from every corner of the world," the Dragon said. "And at last I have the final piece."

The last bone that rose up from the hole was larger than the others. Much larger. So big that now Georgia understood why the entropy had spread so far from the Inkheads' warehouse. It was an enormous skull, at least forty feet long, with more than half its length devoted to massive jaws, each tooth the size of a sword and just as sharp. At the base of the snout, eye sockets like two black caves stood beneath a ridge of small, rounded horns. A fan of longer, sharper horns extended from the back of the skull like a crown of daggers. The skull sailed into the sky and affixed itself to the end of the long neck.

Staring up at the completed skeleton, it all suddenly made sense to Georgia. Why the Dragon kept coming back. Why there was always a dragonslayer to fight her. It was as if the world, having been forged in an act of dragonslaying, had been imprinted with the pattern of its creation. A pattern it repeated endlessly through the eons. Marduk and Tiamat, over and over. Fighting forever.

The Dragon stepped off the porch and approached the titanic skeleton.

"Now that the bones are whole once more, I can shed this pathetic body, retake my true form and devour this entire wretched planet. I find it fitting that my triumph will be the last thing the dragonslayer sees, and equally fitting that yours will be the first meat in my new stomach."

Georgia struggled against Egg Foo again. She had to stop the Dragon before it was too late. If she took over the new body, she would be too big to fight and much too powerful to kill.

The meat puppet adjusted its grip, bringing a stiff arm up to her neck. With the other, it reached into its pocket and pulled out a switchblade. One grey thumb hit the button on the hilt, and the blade snapped open. It held the knife against her cheek and tightened its arm around her throat.

The Dragon lifted her heavy claws toward the bones.

Georgia knew she had to act fast. She reached behind her to scratch at the meat puppet's eyes, but only hit the top of its head. A flick of the switchblade made her stop. Her cheek stung, and she felt a drop of blood roll from the cut. Then she realized why she'd missed. Egg Foo was just a small, skinny teenager. She was bigger. Probably weighed a little more, too. If she could get the right leverage . . .

She hooked her foot behind its ankle and yanked its leg out from under it. She fell backward with it, and as she landed on top of it she managed to get free. She rolled off it and saw the switchblade had fallen from its hand. She grabbed the knife and spun toward the parking lot.

The tips of the Dragon's claws sank into one of the gargantuan ribs. Her reptilian face twisted into a look of ecstasy. She was transferring her consciousness into the skeleton the same way she infected and controlled the dead, Georgia realized.

The bones trembled. Dark smoke clouded the space inside the ribcage and began to spread out along the joints and limbs.

Behind her, Georgia heard the meat puppet struggle to its feet. She sprang off the porch and ran for the Dragon. The Dragon turned to her with a hiss, and Georgia jammed the switchblade into her chest. It sliced through her cloak, her skin, and sank almost all the way to the hilt before it stopped. The Dragon screamed and let go of the skeleton. She fell twisting and shrieking to the ground.

Georgia threw herself on top of the Dragon, grabbed the hilt and leaned on it with all her weight, driving the blade deeper. The Dragon spat up a small geyser of blood and kept screaming. Her claws lashed out, slicing the skin on Georgia's shoulders and back. She felt blood dripping down her arms, her spine. *More infection*, she thought, but it didn't matter. She was already infected. It was worth it to see the Dragon suffer. More than worth it.

From the corner of her eye she saw Egg Foo coming at her.

"Don't even try it." She twisted the blade and made the Dragon scream again.

Egg Foo stopped.

"You will not kill me, child," the Dragon said. Blood dribbled from her lipless mouth.

"Guess again." Georgia leaned harder on the knife.

The Dragon sucked air through her teeth. "You will not because I am the only source of what you need. We are the knot, remember? The tangle from which neither can break free."

"You don't have anything I could possibly want," Georgia said.

"Are you so certain? Consider your mythology. The Garden of Eden. What am I if not a serpent?" One claw disappeared into its billowing cloak sleeve, then reappeared a moment later clutching the brown leather pack she'd taken from Georgia's purse. "What is this if not your apple?"

Georgia stared at the pack.

"It sates a hunger in you even I do not understand," the Dragon said. "What, I wonder, will you do to taste it again?"

Georgia's body trembled. Her gut knotted. Her veins felt empty, yearning, as the addiction howled inside her. She fought to control herself, to resist the temptation, but the jones was strong, and more than that, she could feel the infection moving through her system. She didn't have much time before she succumbed and became just another meat puppet.

She could stop it. Just a taste would do. It would curb the infection, quiet the jonesing . . .

She reached for it, but the Dragon moved it out of her reach. "Kill me and you will never have it."

Georgia leaned on the switchblade again. "Give it to me."

Grunting with effort, the Dragon hurled the leather pack over Georgia's head. Georgia watched it sail across the parking lot. It landed beside the burning frame of the patrol car, so close that the pack's edge instantly started to smoke and char.

"No!"

"Fetch," the Dragon said.

Georgia leapt to her feet and ran after it, the Dragon's mocking laughter hanging in the air behind her. She bent to pull the pack away from the fire. Heat seared her arm, curling the downy hairs there. The leather was hot in her hands, but as she backed away with it from the burning car, she saw little damage had been done. She unrolled the pack quickly. Everything was there: the bag of heroin she'd bought from Egg Foo, even the needle she'd jammed into the Dragon's foot. The Dragon had kept it all. An ace up her sleeve.

There was no time to prepare an injection. She'd have to find another way. She lifted the small plastic baggie out of the pack. Should she snort it? Rub it on her wounds? Would that even work?

A laboured grunt made Georgia glance up. The Dragon was back on her feet. She pulled the switchblade from her body and let it drop to the ground. Wheezing, she took a step toward the gigantic skeleton, stumbled, then quickly righted herself. She latched her claws onto the ribcage again.

The dark smoke inside the skeleton continued to spread, resolving itself into muscle and tissue. Organs inflated out of nothing. A wide network of veins and arteries roped out from the massive heart, and then the innards disappeared as a thick, dark red hide spread over the bones, so dark it nearly disappeared against the night sky as it travelled up the immense neck. The sight froze Georgia in place.

Egg Foo appeared suddenly, grabbing for her. She jumped backward, away from it and onto the motel porch. The leather pack slipped from her hand. The meat puppet kept coming, stepping on it. She heard something snap under its weight. The hypodermic. She turned and ran, clutching the bag of heroin tight in her fist.

She glanced over and saw the Dragon slump before of

the titanic beast, now almost fully formed. The Dragon's claws slid out of its hide. Then her body collapsed into dust, leaving the empty brown cloak pooled on the asphalt in front of one enormous, taloned toe.

Georgia skidded to a halt, not sure what had just happened. Was the Dragon dead?

The enormous toe moved. At first only a twitch. Then the whole foot lifted from the ground and came down on top of the cloak. The porch shook with the impact.

Georgia gawked up at the creature. The Dragon's new body. Tiamat reborn. Her mammoth wings unfurled and blocked out the stars. Her immense jaws opened in a roar that tore the air. The roar shook the ground, shattered windows. Georgia put her hands over her ears until it died away.

The head craned down toward her on its long, serpentine neck until Georgia was staring into two yellow eyes the size of boulders, vertical irises narrowing as they focused on her.

"I can feel it," the Dragon said, and her hot breath washed over Georgia like heat from electric coils. "The whole of the cosmos inside me. Such immense power. To destroy as I see fit. It sets me among the gods." She reared back, lifting her head to the sky again. "I *am* a god!"

A cold hand fell on Georgia's shoulder. The meat puppet had caught up to her. It spun her around, tried to grab her by the wrists.

Towering above, the Dragon opened her mouth wide. A column of fire spat out from between her jaws. Georgia kicked the meat puppet away and ran. The blazing column struck the porch where she'd stood, and the front of the motel went up in a raging fire.

Georgia stopped, looked back to see the meat puppet lurching aimlessly like a drunk, its body engulfed in flame. A moment later it collapsed into a fiery heap.

The Dragon snaked her head in Georgia's direction. She turned to run.

And suddenly she couldn't move. Her legs were locked in place. She looked down and saw both of them had turned completely grey. She couldn't feel them anymore. Her legs were dead. The infection had taken them. The Dragon had control.

Her left leg took a step toward the Dragon, then her right. Something resembling a twisted grin played along the Dragon's jaws. Georgia struggled, tried to stop walking, but she was powerless against it. She still had feeling from the waist up, could still move her arms, but for how much longer? She already felt the infection spreading like ice water from the cuts on her back and shoulders.

"Come to me," the Dragon said.

Her legs carried her relentlessly forward.

The Dragon's head swooped down, her mouth opening.

In the flickering light of the motel fire, Georgia saw countless teeth arranged in sharp rows all the way back to her throat.

Georgia took a deep breath, steeling herself. There would be no flinching this time. No crying or begging for mercy. She wouldn't even give the Dragon the pleasure of hearing her scream.

The visions came, as they always did when the Dragon was about to feed. In her mind, she was looking down from the Dragon's vantage at herself. She looked so small. She saw her own terrified face. She saw slate grey skin. She saw something glisten in her fist.

The bag of heroin. Inside, the brown powder looked as sweet as cocoa mix. It looked so tiny in her palm, too insignificant to have created such a vast need inside her. And yet, how much of her life had she devoted to it? How much time had she wasted in the needle's embrace?

The Dragon's eyes rolled back in her head as she prepared to snap her jaws.

She wished she had Saint George's lance. She'd shove it right down the Dragon's throat.

Her legs carried her another step closer.

She imagined herself in Saint George's place, the King of Cyrene handing her the lance with which to kill the Dragon. No, it wasn't just a simple lance, she remembered. It had been coated with the oil of a local flower. The only thing in the entire kingdom the Dragon wouldn't devour. A flower whose name was lost to time.

She thought back to the Inkheads' warehouse. Stabbing the Dragon's foot with the needle—her own version of the lance. It shouldn't have done anything to the Dragon beyond a moment of pain and shock, yet it had caused her excruciating agony. So much that the Dragon had fled screaming.

Another step.

Georgia thought back to the roadside diner outside Buckshot Hill and something the Dragon said there: *"When*

CHASING THE DRAGON

I tore you open, your blood stung me. It burned."

Another step.

She looked at the bag in her hand. She'd had heroin in her blood when the Dragon mauled her hip. Heroin had kept the ensuing infection in check. Heroin had still been in the tip of the needle when she'd stabbed the Dragon with it.

She realized then what the King of Cyrene's mysterious flower had been. They'd spread poppy oil on Saint George's lance to kill the Dragon.

Opium.

She looked into the Dragon's gargantuan mouth and got the sudden sense that she wasn't alone. Scores of men stood just behind her. Saint George in his black armour. Generations of her ancestors. Her father. They were all there with her. Watching.

Her legs took one last step forward. Right up to the Dragon's chin. Hot breath singed her skin, the tang of burning rock thick in her nostrils.

She opened the plastic bag and threw it into the Dragon's mouth. The heroin spilled out onto her leathery black tongue like confectioner's sugar.

Georgia yanked her hand back as the Dragon's jaws snapped closed. The enormous yellow eyes opened and fixed Georgia with a confused, angry look.

The Dragon bucked suddenly, and her immense wings twitched. Brown foam spurted from the corners of her mouth, seeped from between her teeth, from her nostrils and the corners of her eyes. She squirmed and shook, her tail knocking down trees and telephone poles along the road. Her eyes went wide. The Dragon looked frightened, something Georgia had never seen before.

"The first hit is always the best," she said.

Georgia's arms reached up suddenly, and her fingers wrapped around her own throat. Squeezed. She looked with horror at her arms, saw only black veins running under grey skin. The Dragon had taken control. Georgia tried to suck air into her lungs, but her fingers were squeezing her trachea too tightly. Her vision turned black and fuzzy around the edges. She felt her strength ebbing away, leaking from her like blood from a wound. She fell to her knees, then down on her side. Her fingers kept squeezing, squeezing . . .

The Dragon tried to roar, or maybe she was laughing at Georgia, though what came out was only a laboured wheeze. More brown foam spat from her mouth.

Georgia rolled onto her back as her brain started to shut down, starved for oxygen. Above, the stars were hidden behind massive red wings that shuddered spastically. The leathery skin of the wings tore suddenly from the bones, snapping like ruptured sails.

Then the Dragon did roar, a miserable, pain-wracked scream, loud and terrible enough to split the world in two, and as Georgia struggled for breath, she saw the Dragon wither. Her hide, her organs, they crumbled away into the dust from which they had come, and as Georgia's eyes closed and the scream faded away, she heard the lifeless bones of the Dragon come down. They fell all around her, smashing the cars in the parking lot, demolishing the burning motel porch, and then something fell on Georgia's chest and she didn't hear anything more.

She felt herself falling through the ground and into the earth. Kept falling through darkness.

"Miss?" The voice came out of the black void that surrounded her.

"Miss, can you hear me?" She felt hands around her wrists, felt herself being dragged out from under the debris. A blur of light and colour. Billowing smoke came into focus above her, a half-destroyed neon sign with lights that said only VACANCY for a moment, then flickered out altogether, and she realized she'd opened her eyes. Someone was pulling her by the arms. She felt the heat of a fire nearby, tasted ash in the back of her throat, coughed smoke out of her lungs. She was breathing.

Whoever it was pulled her far away from the burning porch and the still smouldering wreckage of the patrol car, far away from the epicentre of the field of broken, shattered bones, all the way to the end of the building. In the lot outside the motel office, she felt her wrists released. Her arms dropped to the ground, and someone leaned over her, a teenaged boy with acne on his face and braces on his teeth. He looked terrified and confused.

"Wilbur?" she breathed.

"You can hear me?" His face exploded in a big grin of relief. "You can hear me!"

"I can hear you," she said.

"Oh God . . . oh God . . . I thought you were dead." He knelt beside her, helped her sit up. "I called 911. They're sending an ambulance. I . . . I didn't know what else to do."

Georgia coughed again. Her ribs hurt where the bones had fallen on her. Why was she still alive? If nothing else, the infection should have killed her by now.

"Things got so crazy," Wilbur continued, his voice high with panic. "There were so many people, but they weren't people, they were all fucked up, and I hid in the back room of the office. I ... I saw what happened to my dad ... That *thing* ..." His eyes welled with tears. "It killed my dad . . ."

Georgia nodded. "Mine too."

She looked down at herself and saw pink skin on her arms and legs. Bruised, bloody, but pink. She pulled at her waistband and saw the grey was gone even around the wound on her hip.

The infection was gone. As a living part of the Dragon, it had died with her.

It sank in then that she'd done it. She'd actually done something none of her ancestors had, not even Saint George himself. She'd killed the Dragon.

No, she'd done two things they hadn't.

She'd also survived.

She felt Wilbur's body hitch and knew he was trying not to cry in front of her. They leaned against each other and sat on the pavement for a long, quiet moment, watching the motel burn. She heard the pop-pop-pop of the last of her shotgun shells exploding in the room. Somewhere in the conflagration was her broken hypodermic needle. So easy to fix with duct tape, but the fire would have taken it by now. She tensed up. She still wanted the drug. She didn't need it anymore now that the infection was gone, but the ache for it was still there. Just one hit, she thought. To take the edge off. Dull the pain.

"My mom's coming home," Wilbur said. His voice cracked with a sob. "She . . . she was in Santa Fe. I told her what happened. I told her about Dad. How everyone's dead." He shook his head. "I don't know how you survived. I thought for sure you were dead, but I couldn't just leave you there. You're one lucky girl."

"My family," she said. "We're built strong that way."

Exhausted, she asked if she could lie down. Wilbur crossed his legs, and she leaned back until her head rested in the crook of his shins like a pillow.

"When I called my mom, she cried," Wilbur said. "I never heard her cry before. She said she was just glad I was okay. She kept saying it over and over. Over and over. And the weird thing is, I didn't want her to stop."

Georgia looked up at the roiling smoke in the sky. Wilbur was lucky. She wished she could call her parents too and let them know she was okay. She hoped wherever they were, they knew.

Above her, a breeze parted the smoke and she could see the stars again.

EPILOGUE

Georgia's breath clouded before her in the cold Alaskan air. She stopped hiking to catch her breath. She looked at the snow-capped peak of Mount Redoubt looming above her, then turned to see how far she'd come. Below, she saw an oil field with tall metal derricks straddling the wells and drilling rigs moving along the earth like tiny ants between the pipelines and the bobbing arms of the pump jacks. Halfway up, give or take, she thought. It wouldn't be too much longer. Redoubt wasn't particularly steep, but it was massive, nearly ten thousand feet tall over a span of five miles. She took a deep breath, rubbed her gloved hands together and started her ascent again.

Redoubt. It was a fitting name. A stronghold. A secret and protected place.

Wilbur and his mother, Edith, had been waiting for her when she left the hospital the day after the battle at the motel.

CHASING THE DRAGON

They took her in, letting her stay in the guest room of their small house in Buckshot Hill while she recovered. It took nearly a month. In that time, she and Wilbur never told Edith about the Dragon. As far as Edith knew, neither of them had seen anything in the chaos. It was the same story they told the police, and since the fire had erased her prints from the shotgun, they had no reason to doubt their story, choosing instead to focus their investigation on a possible gang war between the Inkheads and the Shaolin Tong.

The lie was a silent agreement between Georgia and Wilbur. They knew no one would understand or believe them. But in Wilbur Georgia had someone with whom she could finally share the burden of truth, and that felt as good as she always thought it would.

As luck would have it, the prolonged investigation kept Edith from demolishing the wrecked motel and removing the rubble from the parking lot. Every night after Edith turned in early, exhausted from her meetings with lawyers, insurance agents and the police, Georgia and Wilbur would sneak back to the motel, duck under the yellow police tape that surrounded the property, and collect as many fragments of Tiamat's shattered bones as they could. They brought them back to the house and stored them in a series of large trunks in the basement. If the fragments were too big to fit, they took great pleasure in smashing them with a sledgehammer.

Georgia stopped again to rest. The air was getting thinner as she approached the summit, and she felt hot in her thick parka. When she'd caught her breath, she started again.

It turned out the friends that Edith Dalton had been

visiting in Santa Fe worked for an international airline company. When Georgia was fully recovered, they generously arranged a job for her as flight attendant. The uniform she had to wear was ridiculous, and it didn't take long for her to develop a hatred for the passengers, but the job took her all over the world. Took her to distant countries where she found deep gorges, tar pits, swamps and caverns that suited her purposes.

When Georgia reached the peak of Mount Redoubt, the thin air grew tinged with a heavy sulphuric odour. She pulled her scarf over her nose and mouth, and strapped on plastic goggles to protect her eyes from the steam that belched out of the wide crater before her.

Redoubt hadn't erupted since 1989, and its gases weren't at a toxic level, but she felt nervous standing so close to the crater of an active volcano. She didn't want to be there any longer than necessary. She reached into the pocket of her parka.

The Dragon would come again, she knew. The earth would spit her out again as surely as it spat out the oil in the field below. The Dragon would be reborn in another age, another civilization with its own dragonslayer. And if that dragonslayer should fail, if the Dragon should live long enough to remember once more who she was, if she should go looking . . . well, Georgia wasn't going to make it easy for her.

From her pocket she pulled a bone fragment smaller than her palm, chipped around the edges and brown on one end from the fire. She didn't know which part of the skeleton it had belonged to. She'd long ago stopped trying to remember what each bone was.

Georgia tossed it as hard as she could. It flew in a long arc above the crater and then disappeared into the steam.

It was dark by the time she reached the base again, where her rental car was waiting. It drove smoother than her father's, but she missed the old Impala anyway. It had been the last thing of her parents' she'd owned, but it had taken too much damage to repair.

She started the car. It would take her several hours to get back to the airport hotel in Anchorage, and that was only if she got lucky and there were no snowstorms. Driving through the streets of the oil workers' village to get back to the main road, she saw houses and barracks painted bright gaudy colours so they could be spotted in a blizzard. After the houses came the bars, big wooden shacks with neon signs in the windows advertising different kinds of beer. The sidewalks outside were packed with bearded men in rough parkas and, sauntering among them, women wearing much too little for such cold weather.

Prostitutes. The oil companies turned a blind eye to it, knowing how far the oil field was from civilization and how lonely the workers, almost entirely male, would get. She'd heard rumours that sometimes the companies themselves surreptitiously flew in prostitutes to keep everyone happy and in line.

Prostitution wasn't the only thing the companies pretended not to notice. Georgia saw shifty men mixing with the workers, taking money from them and handing them bags of weed.

The traffic light at the corner turned red. Georgia stopped and watched the drug dealers until one of them noticed her. A smile cracked his heavily bearded face, and he walked toward her car.

"Hey there, sweetheart," he called through the window. "Always nice to see a new face, 'specially one as pretty as yours. Whaddaya need? Weed, meth, crank, coke, horse?" He tapped the window. "I got a real sweet Mexican black tar, just in from south of the border. I can set you up cheap."

The light turned green.

This time, Georgia drove on.

ABOUT THE AUTHOR

NICHOLAS KAUFMANN

Nicholas Kaufmann is the Bram Stoker Award-nominated author of *General Slocum's Gold*, *Hunt at World's End*, and the short story collection *Walk in Shadows*. His fiction has appeared in *Cemetery Dance*, *The Mammoth Book of Best New Erotica 3*, *City Slab*, *The Best American Erotica 2007*, *Playboy*, *Shivers V*, and others. In addition to writing the monthly "Dead Air" column for *The Internet Review of Science Fiction*, his non-fiction has appeared in the Writers Digest book *On Writing Horror*, *Dark Scribe Magazine*, *Annabelle Magazine*, *Fantastic Metropolis*, *Fear Zone*, and others. He has served on the Board of Trustees for the Horror Writers Association and is a member of the International Thriller Writers. He lives in Brooklyn, NY.

Visit him on the Web at www.nicholaskaufmann.com.